WITCHFUL SHRINKING

A MIDLIFE COZY FANTASY

MIDLIFE AT THE MAGNOLIA
BOOK ONE

JEN LASSALLE

Cover by: Maria Spada Designs

Editing by: Mighty Oak Publishing Services

CHAPTER ONE

A six-foot tall wolf I haven't seen in thirty years smiled at me from the doorway of my musty office.

"Hey, Simone."

My head snapped up off my desk. I blinked at least a dozen times, rubbing crusty sleep out of my eyes and begging my brain to wake the hell up. He kept talking, his lips forming sounds that seemed a lot like words.

I gaped at him, my mouth drier than a week-old muffin, which the amplified grumbling of my stomach told me I would totally eat if it were on a plate in front of me.

A wolf. Talking to me. On a Thursday.

Maybe I was still asleep. Maybe I'd slipped straight from afternoon nap to trauma-induced coma. Given that I'd spent the last six days glued to this exact spot, alternating between sobbing hysterically and screaming at the universe, anything was possible.

Memories from my pre-college life leaked out of my subconscious every time I laid my head down lately. It made sense they'd manifest in the form of an old friend. Who may or may not be a giant dog. That had to be it. I was having another weird dream. Just one more step toward madness.

"Simone?" The wolfman's words broke through my rambling musings. Thick brows furrowed over warm brown eyes. He took a cautious step closer. "CC, are you okay?"

Hearing my old nickname wrenched away the last dregs of my sleep-induced fog. I most definitely would not dream about being called CC again. Even I wouldn't be that cruel to myself.

There was a crick in my neck bigger than the Gulf of Mexico, so I peered at him sideways through one half-open eye until I could see him more clearly. It was not an animal. Silly Simone. It was just a man.

A muscle-packed, broad-shouldered, expensive-suit-wearing hulk of a man.

"Hey," I managed. "I know you." I stood up too fast, my body protesting the movement by barraging my left hip with an army of pins and needles. Rather than fight back, my leg surrendered, and I crumpled into my crappy mesh chair. It slid away as if sick of me, rolling against the wall behind me. I sort of hovered mid-air, half my butt in the seat.

"I'm gonna need a minute." I held up one finger, rubbing at my angry hip joint with a balled fist and mentally clawing his name out of the back of my brain. It was embarrassing enough he'd caught me sleeping at work. I wasn't about to admit I only half-remembered him.

Although, to be fair, I couldn't remember much of anything these days. Not that I was in the habit of being fair to myself, but given what I was going through, surely I could manage the smallest bit of slack. In the past week, my life had been flipped inside out and dumped upside down. I was a junk drawer of a mess right now, so the name of my old running buddy wasn't exactly at the tip of my tongue.

Old running buddy! Could remembering that be enough of a win? Probably not. I scrunched my eyes closed and flipped through my mental rolodex—my brain would never go digital—until I came up with his file. Finally, a name floated to the surface.

"Ethan?" I managed to stand and round the desk then hobbled closer to greet him, extending a hand I prayed didn't have dried chocolate on it. "My goodness, I haven't seen you since high school."

That wasn't entirely true. While I hadn't seen him in person, the tight-end-turned-attorney's wide smile was once plastered across every billboard in the greater New Orleans area. His confident voice had been the start of every commercial interruption on football Sundays for years.

"Ethan Mosely. Leading the Pack in Louisiana Justice." I lifted my head to grin at him. At only five feet, I usually had to look up at people. But Ethan straight up towered over me. "You're still tall."

"Long time, CC." He dipped his chin, tightly coiled curls teasing his eyebrows and the tops of his ears. "How have you been? You look great."

I held his gaze for a moment, trying to read his emotions for sincerity. Yep, he meant it. He thought I looked great. My mother had always called my ability to tell what a person was feeling borderline supernatural, but I figured I just read subtle cues better than other people. Either way, it was nice to know I didn't look like a swamp rat. At least in his eyes.

"Come on in, and I'll tell ya." He followed me toward the desk, taking the single comfy chair I kept across from it while I slid back into my mesh menace. "Can I get you anything to drink? Coffee or tea? Water?"

It was silly to offer it once I'd already sat down, and even sillier because I didn't have anything to offer. I scanned the array of paper food bags overflowing from the small trash can beside my desk and the thin layer of grime covering the shelf on the opposite wall. Plenty of junk and self-help books. Not a clean cup in sight. Definitely no coffee or tea.

Yep. I had nothing to offer.

"I'm covered, thanks." He opened the briefcase I hadn't noticed he carried and extracted a massive thermos. It was more battered than a war tank and a hideously bright shade of orange you could see from space. It bore the logo of our high school alma mater. He unscrewed the lid and leaned back, propping his foot on the opposite knee while he took a sip.

"I can't believe you still carry that thing." My sudden laugh lightened the load on my shoulders. Strange memories from my youth had been surfacing more often than I cared to admit lately. His goofy grin and stupid thermos were a reminder they weren't all terrible.

Despite our awkward start, it was nice to see a familiar face. Still, a cold prick of panic tapped at my throat as the situation settled over me. I didn't have any appointments on my calendar. I didn't even have a calendar anymore. It wasn't going to be long before my landlord showed up and shut down my failing business.

So why was an attorney in my office?

"How's the personal injury biz these days?" I kept my voice even, adrenaline surging through me. He seemed genuinely happy to see me, but there was a sense of nervousness in the way he avoided eye contact. My now-wide-awake instincts shouted a warning. This was not a social visit. "Was I unfairly injured in a car wreck and don't know it?"

"Oh no, I'm just Ethan Mosely now." His embarrassed chuckle filled the room, but it did nothing to soothe my concerns. "I gave up ambulance-chasing five years ago and moved back home. I'm in family law now."

Family law. My stomach twisted itself into a giant knot.

"I see." I swallowed down the urge to throw up. Why was hurling always my default when I was upset? "You're here because you're Jeff's attorney."

Any goodwill I'd managed earlier dissipated. It was a cheap trick for that bastard husband of mine to hire someone from the hometown I'd fought so hard to forget. In the week since we split, I'd done little more than drown my sorrows in junk food and reality TV.

I'd wallowed. Meanwhile, Jeff already had a divorce lawyer with a fierce reputation and an emotional connection to me. No wonder he'd barely managed to send his estranged wife a few texts and calls but never come to find me. He was already planning his escape. As if he were the one who needed escaping.

"You can tell your client to go straight to hell, Ethan." A dam of tears threatened to burst behind my eyes. Pressure built in my throat. "I hope that cheating pile of dirt finds vomit in every pair of shoes he touches."

"Go straight to hell?" Ethan clasped his hand over his mouth, and his eyes grew about three sizes. He was looking at me like I had sprouts growing out of my ears. "Vomit in shoes, CC? What are you talking about?"

"Well, that's what I did when I caught him in bed with another woman. I hope he told you that part when he hired you, because it sure makes trying to squeeze the nothing I have left out of me even harder." My voice was becoming more shrill by the word. I wanted to stand, to kick Ethan's perfectly round ass out of my office, but I was rooted to the chair I'd slept in since I left my house.

My heart was pounding ten miles a minute against my chest. I pressed my lips together and bit down on the inside of my cheek to keep the world from swimming around me. If I didn't get it together, I was headed toward a breakdown. What's worse, I was gonna going to lose it in front of a put-together old friend.

What would I tell one of my patients right now to help them? My mind was blank. It had been so long since I'd treated a panic attack that I didn't know the answer. I wasn't a great therapist on the best of days, let alone under duress. My dust-filled, coffee-devoid office was a testament to that.

Aside from Ethan, I'd only seen one other person in the past week and that had led to disaster. A strange woman who rushed into my office for an unscheduled session. I'd fumbled my way through her bizarre issue, which left me with a throbbing headache impossible to ignore.

I'd gone home early, rather than manage the pain in my empty office.

That's when I walked in on my husband having sex with his physical therapist.

"CC." It took several minutes for me to register that Ethan was saying my name. I squinted at him, hoping to sharpen my focus. "CC, can you look at me? Can you take a deep breath?"

My throat was burning like I'd swallowed fire. All I wanted was to go back to my wallowing. Or to dive into the bag of emotional support M&M's I kept in my top drawer. I fixed my eyes on him, attempting a very weak glare.

"What?"

"I'm not Jeff's attorney. I'm not here because of him." He reached across the desk, his large hands covering my fingers, which I'd been weaving in and out while my emotions spiraled. "I don't even know who Jeff is, sweetie. If anything, I'm kind of *your* attorney now."

Oh. His thumb stroked a path along my hand, and I let myself focus on it, willing my body to breathe again. The nausea in my belly was replaced by a warm flush of embarrassment that clawed its way up my neck and into my cheeks. After a very long moment of tense silence, I extracted my hands from his and pressed my palms tight against my eyes.

"I'm sorry. I'm not in the best of places right now."

"Don't sweat it, CC. I've been through a few divorces myself."

"A few, huh?" I lowered my hands to look at him, relieved to find his joking smile waiting for me. He slid his thermos toward me, and I took it with a nod of thanks, drinking down the bulk of the contents until my belly jostled.

I wasn't okay. Nowhere near it. Not only had I made a fool of myself, but I'd massively overshared. Plus, Ethan had said the d-word. Despite Jeff's infidelity, I hadn't reached that conclusion. I was at a complete and total loss as to what to do next. I wasn't thinking divorce. At least not yet.

I was headed to a bad place. And a hotter-than-hot local celebrity lawyer had a front row ticket to my downfall. Awesome.

Wait. What did he mean he was *my* attorney?

To hell with it. I opened my desk and dug into the candy bag.

"So, why are you here?" I shoveled the perfect chocolate morsels into my mouth and chewed. "Not that it isn't nice to see you, but, you know, it's been thirty years without so much as a social media ping."

"That it has." Ethan's gaze lingered for a moment, then he hefted his briefcase onto his lap.

Most of high school was a distant memory. The therapist part of me had long ago surmised it was my coping mechanism. I'd shut down all thoughts of the quaint hometown where I grew up rather than deal with the trauma of losing my mother and having my heart shattered senior year. The one-two punch had been enough to send me packing, never to return or think about Treater's Way again. It was only thirty miles from my home in New Orleans. Might as well have been three-hundred.

What I knew for sure was that Ethan and I never dated. We'd never been anything more than casual friends with a mutual interest in working out that led to a few mornings a week in the gym or a race around the track.

Still, if it weren't for the fact that I hadn't showered in who-knows-how-long and probably looked borderline homeless, I might have thought there was longing in the way he admired me. And that, above everything else, had me wondering why he was here. And just how bad I looked.

I excused myself and rushed to the bathroom. I rummaged through the cabinet until I found a travel pack of toothpaste and a toothbrush. I scrubbed sleep out of my eyes and ran damp fingers through my mess of knots.

A few months ago, I'd cut my long brown curls into a sort of wavy blunt bob. It hit just above my shoulders and framed my face. Even I could admit I looked younger than my actual age of forty-eight. I wasn't exactly getting carded these days, but I wasn't in the "old people are unattractive camp" and never had been. To my mind, age was not a factor when evaluating beauty.

Sure, I focused a bit too much on those tiny lines around my eyes.

And my eyelids drooped heavier than they had in my twenties. Nothing a little makeup couldn't fix ... if I chose to wear it. But all in all, I was doing okay in the looks department.

Besides, I didn't mind looking middle-aged.

I wasn't a fan of feeling it though.

Once I was sure I looked moderately passable, I returned to my office.

"What's this?" A file folder sat on the desk between my chair and Ethan's. I picked it up and opened it as I took my seat.

"That's why I'm here." Ethan clicked a pen and pointed at the paper with it. "Do you remember Agatha Dupree? She owned the Magnolia Therapy Center?"

"Of course. There's no way I could forget Agatha." Despite what I'd said, I hadn't thought of Agatha in years. But the mention of her name sent a flood of memories through me. Suddenly, I could picture her as if she were standing next to us.

"Salt-and-pepper hair that tangled its way down to her waist. Leathery skin from too many carefree days in the sun. And a smile that made you feel so doggone safe." I closed my eyes, breathing in the sensation of her warm hugs and the welcoming scent of the banana bread she loved to bake. "My mom always said she couldn't have asked for a better boss. And she was like a grandmother to me."

A cool breeze stroked my hair and ran down my arm. For just a moment, I could believe she was actually here, soothing me now the way she had when my mother died. Guilt clamped my heart like a vice. When I'd left town, I'd left Agatha behind. I opened my eyes to find Ethan's brimmed with tears, grief a dark shroud surrounding him. Everyone in town loved Agatha.

"She's gone, isn't she?" The air in the room crackled, as if a vital source of energy was shut off, and a pain I hadn't felt since I was eighteen landed in my stomach like a poisoned lead brick. I looked down at the papers Ethan's now-trembling fingers pointed toward. *Last Will and Testament of Agatha Cecelia Dupree.*

"I'm afraid so. Agatha passed peacefully in her sleep last Friday." Ethan's voice quivered. He cleared his throat, shifting in his chair. For a moment, the brush of skin against leather was the only sound in the room. Then Ethan tapped his pen back to the paper. "You've inherited the Magnolia House."

I jolted in my desk, certain I'd heard him wrong. "Why would she do that?"

"I can't say," he shrugged his shoulder a little too casually. "Whatever her motivations were, the will is very clear."

I scanned the papers, barely reading the words. He wasn't kidding. The room was quiet again. Too quiet. No wood creaked. No car revved an engine outside. I was in a bubble of disbelief, and only his words cut through the deafening silence.

"It's not just the house, Simone. She left you everything."

CHAPTER TWO

The Magnolia House needed some work. Well, that was a generous way of wording it. The house was a run-down piece of crap.

A grubby post-storm haze clung to the windowpanes. The house had once been a soft, lovely yellow. But time and weather had faded the color and chipped the paint. Instead of a soothing pastel, the house appeared sickly. Sage green shutters hung off their hinges, relying on weed-ridden flower boxes to keep them in place.

Rust rained down from the wrought-iron railing bordering the second floor, an ornate design of fleur-de-lis and the namesake flower. It dusted the top of the warped, faded sign swinging below it.

Magnolia Therapy ~~Clinic~~ and Wellness Center.

Someone had actually struck through the word clinic with a black marker and hand-written the rest of the sign.

This did not bode well for what I would find inside. Though the lawn was freshly mowed, the hedges were overgrown, and the sidewalk hadn't seen a pressure wash in a hot minute.

It was an eyesore of epic proportions. And it was all mine.

Well, technically it wasn't. Not yet. Once I'd lifted my jaw off the floor, Ethan had explained that I had a thirty-day trial period to decide whether to accept my inheritance. During that time, I was expected to establish myself as the head of the therapy division and accept ownership of the organization as well as the house.

Whatever that meant.

I'd been bequeathed a dilapidated mansion and a failing business. But at least I had a roof over my head for the next month. Even if that roof leaked. I figured as long as there was a bed, it was already a step up from sleeping at my desk.

A dark cloud hung behind the house, threatening rain. I needed to get inside and get away from dark, scary thoughts. It wasn't like me to dwell on the negative. I wasn't about to start now.

The house was still the same gorgeous structure that greeted me each day when I'd walked from school to see my mom. The business couldn't be any worse than the one I'd left back in New Orleans. It needed a bit of work. Maybe some love. But hey ... so did I.

Either way, I was likely on the verge of bankruptcy.

If I got a new sign, met with the division heads, and understood the operations better, I could probably turn it around if I tried. How bad could it be?

I paused my thoughts there, rubbing a fist to my heart. A small trickle of excitement flared. I hadn't even bothered to take a polish rag to the desks in my clinic. So why did this house feel worth putting effort into? Maybe the OG Simone was still buried under layers of despondence.

"I'm going to be excited about this. This is a positive change in the right direction. Clouds may come, and storms may rage, but they will pass. I will receive a sign that this is going to work out."

I wasn't much one for toxic positivity, but choosing to focus on the bright side out loud did make me feel better. As if it agreed, the storm cloud dissipated, and the sky brightened.

Weird, but I would take it.

The front door opened with a groan, and a woman stepped out. She had the kindest smile I'd ever seen. Her straw-blond hair fell below her shoulders in cute, blunt layers. Her makeup was minimal but tasteful, and the peachy tint to her skin made me think of fresh fruit and picnics. The straight, loose yellow dress she wore completed the effect. This woman embodied all the best parts of summer. Her awkward little wave charmed me.

"Are you going to come in? I promise anyone that might bite you isn't here today."

I had to laugh at the strange wording. Whoever she was, she had an aura that soothed me, like I was about to meet my very best friend. Maybe this was my sign.

"Sorry," I called out, still lingering on the sidewalk. "I was sitting with my emotions. Well, technically I was standing with them."

Her smile softened, and a sympathetic gleam lit her green eyes.

"Yep, you're a therapist all right. Come on in, Simone. We're so glad you're here."

I took a deep breath, mostly because I was picturing myself in a movie moment and that was what the main character did before embarking on a big journey. And that thought, that I was the main character in my own life again, was the last step I needed to move forward. I stepped onto the busted, cobbled path leading to the Magnolia House and walked forward.

When I reached the woman, I stuck my hand out.

"Simone Bardot. Nice to meet you."

She pulled me forward into a hug.

"Girl, this is the South, and you and I are already besties. Can't you feel it? Besties gotta hug!" She said the last bit in a funny whine that reminded me of the movie *Tommy Boy*. I had to appreciate a goofy sense of humor. With her friendly embrace, the remainder of my tension dissolved.

"So good to be back in a small town, I gotta say."

"It's the place for me, no doubt." She opened the door, and I followed her inside. "I was born and raised in Atlanta but got here just as quick as I could.

"I'm Brianne Steele, by the way." She continued forward, toward the open-door kitchenette peeking out from the back of the main area. "You want coffee? Some tea, maybe?"

I barely heard her name. I'd stopped walking when I reached the lobby, and my mouth hung open. The inside of the Magnolia didn't look anything like the outside. And it was very, very different from when my mom had worked here thirty years ago.

Natural sunlight flooded down from a skylight so far above me I had to crane my neck to see it. Strange, as the house hadn't seemed that tall from the outside. A wrought-iron balcony, with the same design but polished to a gleam, overlooked the main lobby. I couldn't see anything beyond that on the upper floor.

The lobby was long and narrow, with wide-board oak floors and walls a soothing shade of warm gray. A few chairs and a floral rug adorned the center. On each side were two sets of doors. The doors were a dark mahogany, with unique carvings and simple yet tasteful signs next to brass doorbells.

Past the doors was a small corner office, squared off by a matching floral rug. There were no walls other than the one behind the desk, which was covered with two large white bookshelves and a massive filing cabinet. Still, it felt like its own space.

The rustic desk matched the bookshelves and was sparsely covered. A sleek phone sat in one corner with a laptop in the center. The only pops of color were a high-backed, bright pink desk chair and a large bouquet of red roses sitting atop the file cabinet.

The entire area had a clean and simple feel to it, yet it was warm and inviting. There were no scents in the crisp air. Had I been tense when I arrived? That was all gone now. I wanted to relax in this lobby.

"It's so different." I gratefully accepted the glass of iced coffee Brianne handed me.

"I've had a hand in redecorating over the years. I hope you don't mind."

"Why would I?" I wandered closer to the first door on my right. An intricate series of swirls were carved onto the front, reminding me of hair flowing in the breeze. The sign, in simple, bold charcoal lettering, read SALON.

"Well, I took over after your mother passed."

I pivoted to face Brianne.

"You've worked here for thirty years?"

"Not exactly." An edge of unsureness was working through Brianne's voice. "Agatha kept your mother's position open until about twenty years ago when my husband and I moved here. I have to say, the records and operations manuals your mom created were impeccable. She could have run this place with her eyes closed."

My eyes welled at the naked admiration in her voice. I didn't think about my mother a lot. It hurt too much. It was nice to know she was still well-remembered.

Brianne lifted her lips into a quirky half-smile. "But her taste in decor was a little, shall we say, basic?"

I closed my eyes, as much to keep the tears in check as to visualize the lobby the way it used to look. I could have sworn there were only two doors at the time, but I must be remembering it wrong. It's not like they could have added rooms.

Which was odd, too, because as narrow as the lobby was, it also seemed to be the same width as the house. From the outside, it didn't appear to have space for four rooms on each end. They would have to be tiny.

What I could envision from the past was sparse furniture, most of which came in a box and required assembly. I chuckled to myself at the memory of the dozen or so tiny Allen wrenches Mom had kept in a drawer in our kitchen, just in case one of the boxes didn't include its own.

"We didn't have money when I was growing up. My dad wasn't around, and Mom worked hard. I know Agatha asked her to make the place look presentable, but Mom couldn't get over the expense."

I wanted to soothe Brianne and make sure she understood I had no resentful feelings about the changes she'd made. Time moved on, whether we wanted it to or not. I liked Brianne on sight and knew I would enjoy working with her. It was painful to admit, but I was starving for friendship.

Still, it occurred to me that I was her boss now. Or I would be, if this worked out. I wanted us on the right footing.

"Everything looks beautiful. It feels clean and welcoming and soothing, just like the Magnolia should." I flipped my coffee to my left hand and wiped the condensation on my slacks, then reached out to shake her hand. "I have absolute faith in your ability to manage the Magnolia, Brianne. You're meant to do great things here."

It was another odd thing to say, but I was used to being awkward on first meetings. And sometimes second meetings. And, if the other person was really pretty, really tall, or had that cool vibe ... well, it took me a long time to fully get over the awkwardness. Sometimes it stayed forever.

Brianne's smile was warm and held a hint of approval that relaxed all the pieces inside me that wanted to look cool in front of her or impress her. Bypassing my hand once more, she grabbed me into a quick side hug.

"I think we're both going to do great things, Simone." She released me, then scurried over to her desk and pressed a few buttons on the phone before grabbing a manila envelope from the bottom drawer. It was then that she looked at me and furrowed her brow, searching around me as much as she was staring at me.

It brought the awkward sensation rushing back. I replayed our conversation in my head to find the moment I'd said something wrong. Something in my welcome or my words had just landed with her, and an uneasy feeling settled in my stomach, turning the coffee from refreshing to bitter. What had I said wrong?

"Where's your luggage?" She went to the front door and opened it, scanning the patio. "Did Ethan explain that there's lodging upstairs? And that you're required to live in it?"

"Oh, that. He said there was lodging but I don't have a lot of clothes right now." I fiddled with the edge of my shirt. After Ethan had left, I'd changed into a spare set of clothes in my office and called a rideshare before I could change my mind. Going back to my house to pack hadn't occurred to me. "Ethan told me he'd explain everything after the board meeting."

Brianne was staring at me like I had just told her I planned to raise pet hyenas. My palms were getting clammy, and the hairs on my arms lifted as a sudden wave of heat settled over me. The lobby hadn't been this warm when I walked in, had it? A trickle of sweat formed at the base of my neck and trickled down my spine, landing at the small of my back.

"That wasn't the way that conversation was supposed to go." She twisted her lips, as if trying to decide what to do. Whatever I was missing, it was important. Finally, she shook her head. "We can discuss it with Ethan when he gets here. I wonder why he didn't explain the situation more fully?"

"I think that's my fault." My cheeks felt like they were on fire. I'd started early stages of menopause a few years prior. One of my least favorite side effects was my fun new ability to flush bright red whenever I was embarrassed, awkward, or uncomfortable. Since that was most of the time, I walked around splotchy and red faced. "My husband and I are going through a separation and Ethan caught me at a, well, let's just call it a bad moment."

Brianne set her hand on my arm, the gesture putting me at ease again. I smiled at her understanding gaze, her compassion filling me as if she'd hugged me a third time. I really liked this woman.

A new aroma filled the room, the soothing scent of caramel and vanilla and some kind of spice. Something dinged in the kitchen, and Brianne chuckled.

"That must be for you." She took the iced coffee from my hand, and I followed her to the kitchen where a tall mug sat on a matching coaster, a swirl of steam surrounded the mocha foam layered over the top.

A Bayou Bliss. The non-caffeinated drink my mother used to make for me.

"Oh wow, I haven't had one of those in ages. How did you know?"

Brianne didn't answer. She leaned against the cabinet while I took my first sip. It was like being transported back to my childhood, when I'd read books or sung songs behind my mother's desk while she greeted customers and answered phones. It was my lone treat, every day after school, and I hadn't had one since.

As a child, it had seemed so exotic, having a special drink that was all mine. Sipping it now, I recognized the flavors my mom always claimed came from a "magical place far away" as chai and chocolate with a hint of caramel. And something else. Something very Louisianan.

"Chicory." I laughed at Brianne's raised eyebrows. "It's a decaf chai latte with chocolate, caramel, and chicory. I didn't know that growing up." She lifted her lips in disgust, and I laughed again.

"I've never had a taste for chicory personally." Brianne gestured at the empty cup in the sink. "I like my coffee with a touch of milk and a hint of sugar and not a thing else. And not one minute after two pm, or I will be up all night."

"Hah, I don't think much would keep me up at this point." Weariness settled over me the moment I said it. The combination of the drink and being back at a place I used to call home was smoothing out a part of me long coiled tight. And with that weariness came a deep sadness, as words I didn't know I'd had stored up came tumbling out.

"Last week, I caught my husband cheating on me when I came home early from work. He had a health condition a year ago, a rare disorder that led to emergency surgery and a lot of recovery. Apparently, his physical therapist was really good at her job because he was screwing her in my house."

The words hung in the air, the room somehow getting quieter. My lip trembled. Even a Bayou Bliss couldn't fix this.

But Brianne seemed to know what to do. She gestured to the small, round table in the kitchenette, where we both took a seat.

She shoved a plate of cookies in my direction. "How long were you married?"

"Twenty years." I drew in a shaky breath, trying to release the lump in my throat.

"Kids?"

"One son." I broke off a chunk of a small, pink cookie and fiddled with it just to give my hands something to do. "He's almost twenty."

"I see." To my relief, Brianne didn't pry. Without me saying it outright, she'd understood that Jeff and I got married because I was pregnant and filled in the blanks. And it warmed my heart that her voice was laced with kindness instead of judgment.

"Are you married?" I couldn't remember the last time I'd had a female friend, and though I'd known her all of half-an-hour, it somehow felt natural sitting at the table sharing things with her.

"Twenty-five years this May." Love and joy shined bright in her eyes. A new kind of sadness, raw and envious, pulsed in my heart. Had I ever looked like that when I mentioned Jeff to someone? Probably not. "We've got a brood of our own. I'll introduce you one day."

"I'd like that very much." My stomach grumbled like a lion in search of an antelope. "You know, Brianne, I don't think I've had anything other than sugar to eat in at least a day. And I've been sleeping in my office for a week."

"Well then, why don't we go upstairs so you can have a nice lunch and settle in?"

"As long as I don't have to cook." When Jeff first got sick, well-wishers and colleagues sent casseroles and food delivery gift cards by the dozen. We were still finishing off the contents of our freezer, and I couldn't remember the last time I'd made a meal of my own. Which is a good thing, because I wasn't exactly an ace in the kitchen.

My throat was warm from the drink, and clogged from my random, pitiful thoughts. The one place I should have been an ace was in my therapy clinic. And I hadn't even done that right.

Looking at this put-together woman in front of me, the same age as me but with a life I could tell she enjoyed and work that fulfilled her, I felt like a tiny, messed up possum. It wasn't just my appearance. I could manage disheveled hair and my wrinkled clothes. It was how I felt on the inside. Like my soul was as hungry as my stomach.

Somewhere in the past year, while caring for Jeff and trying to hold together the last dregs of my failing practice, I'd gripped onto everything with my fingertips while letting the rest of my body hang loose. And just the offer of a supportive friend was enough to bring it all to the surface and make me realize everything I'd lost. And everything I'd let go of.

Right there in the lobby of the company that I now owned, with businesses I knew next to nothing about and a complete stranger in front of me, I broke down and gave in to the ugly, black despair I'd ridden on for far too long. Tears erupted like a geyser. A sob escaped my throat, a strange sound that didn't hold my voice, like a cork popping on champagne then ricocheting off the wall.

"Hunh." I clamped one hand over my mouth at the odd sound, searching the space as if a customer had suddenly appeared and I would lose this business, too. "I'm so sorry."

"Oh, honey." Brianne took my hand and led me through the kitchenette and out a door in the back. "Let's get you upstairs."

The backdoor led to a small, fenced-in yard. Overhead was another balcony, with a spiral staircase a short distance to my left. There were no stairs inside the building, which meant this was the only way to the second floor. Given that was supposed to be my new digs, it was reassuring to know I'd have some privacy.

Brianne fished a key from the envelope she'd retrieved earlier and unlocked the door. She stepped aside and gestured toward the doorway. "Welcome home, Simone."

CHAPTER THREE

I'd expected the upstairs to be shotgun-style, like the bottom floor. Instead, a wide, open-concept space greeted me.

To the right was a large but cozy sitting area, with a sleek television and a bold, red couch I couldn't wait to stretch out on and take a nap. On the left was a full kitchen and adjoining breakfast nook. Large bay windows overlooked the backyard and the New Orleans skyline in the distance. We definitely weren't high enough for that to be visible, but the outline was unmistakable. So far away, and yet so close I could still make out the Dome.

In the breakfast nook was a pretty, round, black table made of weathered wood. I didn't know design concepts or names of styles. Was it shaker or contemporary? I would be guessing. But the bulky legs of the table, and the upholstered gray chairs surrounding it, beckoned me.

A heavenly, rich aroma greeted us as we neared the table, where a bowl of vegetable soup and the crispest, most perfect looking grilled cheese sandwich I'd ever seen waited for me to pounce. It took all I had not to lift the bowl to my mouth and gulp it down. Brianne sat opposite me, sipping from a deep blue glass while I inhaled the hearty meal.

"This is the most scrumptious sandwich I've ever eaten." I took a bite, relishing the crunch and ooze of cheese on my tongue. "Sourdough bread. A good, sharp cheddar. Man, I'm in heaven."

Brianne stared at my plate with naked envy. Then, she snatched the other half of my sandwich with enough zeal to make me laugh out loud.

"I don't know how the food stayed warm while we were downstairs, but thank you for making it."

"Oh, I didn't." Brianne winked at me. "This place comes with a personal chef."

"Where are they?" I craned my neck. I didn't remember seeing anyone else. There was no one in the kitchen, and the counters were spotless. They must have cooked, then left. Odd that we didn't pass them on the stairwell. "I can't wait to meet them."

The idea of having a personal chef seemed too decadent for me. And given what the exterior of the house looked like, and the fact that no customer had come in or out of the business while I wept in the lobby, I had concerns about finances. As amazing as this lunch was, I'd have to consider surviving on frozen meals for a while.

We barely talked while I ate, mostly because I was hoovering food like a starving person. I'd been surviving on takeout for a week. Even this simple meal seemed like a five-star feast. When we finished, Brianne took the dishes to the sink, murmuring a quick *thank you* under her breath. She walked to the short hallway and motioned for me to follow.

"Down this way is a bedroom, with a comfortable bed you'll never want to leave. There are toiletries in the bathroom, and I suspect you'll find something to wear in the closet." She took my hand and guided me. "Why don't you have a shower and a nap, or if it were me, I'd have a nap and a shower, and we can talk more later this evening. Your board meeting is at six. That gives you plenty of time to get yourself together. A lot's about to happen, Simone. More than you know, I suspect."

She gave me a fierce hug, then rushed out the door, leaving me suddenly alone. Despite just having met her, I wish she'd stayed. Everything was overwhelming, and while I appreciated her giving me space to process, I had too many questions to rest.

There were a hundred thoughts racing, and a dozen things I wanted to do. Review the copy of the will that Ethan had given me earlier that day. Wander this beautiful space that, despite Agatha being well over a hundred years old, was decorated in a style I could only describe as mine. Go back downstairs and view each of the divisions of the wellness center, get a feel for the clientele, and figure out what therapy and haircuts had to do with one another.

Where did I start? Did I dance around skipping and shouting yippee? I didn't much like dancing these days. I wanted to share the news with someone. I sent a quick text to my son. A text I knew he would ignore. Again.

Maybe I should tell my husband. Maybe Jeff and I could work things out if we moved here together? He had his faults, but if he could help me get the business built ...

I stopped myself. Jeff's betrayal kept landing on me in strange waves. I'd get angry, then heartbroken, then forget all about it. Was that because of this new development? Or was that because, if I looked deep down, I'd have to admit we'd been living somewhat separate lives since his surgery? Catching him cheating had been shocking, but I couldn't say I was surprised our marriage went sideways.

I was too overwhelmed to go down that rabbit hole. He'd called every day while I slept in my office, but not once had he come to see me. My phone held a slew of unread texts and unopened voice notes. I'd finally put him on ignore. Jeff had a way with words, and I didn't trust myself to hear him out. So, for now, I needed to stay away from cheating Jeff and his silver tongue.

"I hope you bite that silver tongue of yours every time you try to use it to lie, Jeffy-poo."

Saying it out loud, no matter how silly, made me feel better. All these bubbles of anger and betrayal were floating inside me, and each time one popped, it released a little bit of the pressure holding me in place.

Man, I was exhausted. Mentally and physically and emotionally weary. And I was standing in the middle of a space that wasn't officially mine but felt like it, letting my internal monologue overwhelm me. I walked the short hallway toward the front of the building, which oddly was the back of my house. There were two rooms. A small office on the left I promised myself I'd look into later and the bedroom I would inhabit for at least the next thirty days.

I turned right, then stopped short to take it in. Wow. How could this be possible?

If I could have designed my dream bedroom, this is what it would look like. There was a gabled ceiling with thick wooden posts that met at the peak. The walls were the softest shade of beige I'd ever seen, except for the accent wall opposite the windows, which was a deep green that made me think of a forest. It soothed the eye, creating this natural, earthy vibe that spoke to my inner wanderlust.

It was sparsely furnished but felt open rather than empty. Aside from the bed, there were simple nightstands, an armoire, and two chests of drawers. The windows were cracked open, allowing in a cool breeze that seemed impossible for the South in mid-July. Even though the windows opened to the town, I couldn't hear any outside noises. Long, sage curtains billowed with the breeze.

It was almost like they pointed at the bed. With butter-like sheets and a mountain of pillows, I couldn't wait to slide into it. Brianne was right ... nap first, shower second. I checked one of the drawers and found a pair of cotton shorts and a matching shirt in my size. In fact, a quick check of the rest of the clothes showed me that all of it was my size. I stopped again and looked around the room.

The more at home I felt, the more certain I was that someone had cleaned this space after Agatha's death and prepared it for me. If she had passed a week earlier, that seemed like a lot of work. Maybe Agatha herself had done it, though I'm not sure how a woman a century old who hadn't seen me in thirty years would know my tastes. *I* didn't even know my tastes.

It was one more thing I needed to understand. After a nap. I dropped my phone on the charging station, set an alarm, and burrowed into the comfiest bed on the entire planet. I was asleep the moment my head hit the pillow.

I awoke before my alarm, feeling like I'd slept for days rather than hours. I stood up to stretch, reaching my arms overhead the way I did every morning. Oddly, my shoulders weren't aching, and my low back wasn't tight. I guess sleeping on the right mattress really did matter. Jeff and I were still using the crappy bed we'd bought fresh out of college. A new mattress had been on my list, but money was a factor, particularly since my business was failing and we were neck-deep in hospital bills.

I put that thought aside. If I had the luxury of thirty days on a comfy mattress that didn't make me wake up feeling like I was nearing ninety instead of fifty, I would take it with gratitude.

The bathroom was just as impressive as the rest of the house. I hated massive bathrooms, where you always felt cold when you stepped out of the shower. This one was the perfect size. With green features that gave it a cohesive flow from the bedroom—and royal purple accents—it was both peaceful and whimsical.

The shower had one of those fancy waterfall heads that pummeled all the tension out of my shoulders. I'd planned to stand under it until the water turned cold. After thirty minutes, my skin was pruning and the water was the same temperature.

Now that my basic needs were met, a whisper of anxiety was sliding into my mind. This board meeting was my first opportunity to meet everyone. How did they feel about Agatha leaving everything to a stranger? If it were me, I'd be upset. Then again, maybe they liked not having the responsibility or the pressure I was beginning to realize was building inside. I'd already run one business into the ground. Did they know that? What *did* they know about me?

I couldn't hide in the shower forever. After toweling off, I inspected the drawers in the massive vanity on the off chance I would find a spare toothbrush.

What I found shouldn't have surprised me. Whoever had taken the time to prepare the bedroom thought of everything. Not only could I brush my teeth, but the drawers were fully stocked with a full line of face and hair products. I inspected the matching labels that read *Magnolia Beauty*. They were the same as the logo downstairs in the lobby. We had a beauty line, too?

The makeup bore the same logo, not that I had any idea what to do with it. I'd always been an *au naturel* kind of person. Not by choice. Mostly, I was inept when it came to anything other than slapping on lipstick and a quick swipe of mascara. Even then, I somehow ended up with black goop under my eyes.

I didn't want to have a heavy, caked-on appearance. But one look in the gold-framed mirror told me that a week of misery was taking its toll. Heavy bags and dull features reflected at me. I could at least look presentable when I met everyone. I hoped.

I grabbed my phone and searched for makeup videos, stopping at the now familiar signature that matched our logo.

Holy cow. We had a YouTube channel with over two million followers!

Scrolling through, most of the videos were from different hosts, so I couldn't be sure who I was about to meet. I found one for a quick, professional look and followed the chirpy, sultry voiced female's instructions. Surveying myself, I actually looked ... right.

Back in the bedroom, I opened the armoire fully expecting to see more clothes that fit me. Sure enough, there was an assortment of sharp slacks and pretty, pastel tops. I ran my fingers along a silky satin blouse the color of a ripe peach, admiring the expensive materials. This couldn't have been Agatha's clothing. Even if she'd shrunk with age, she'd been much taller than me and preferred bohemian-style dresses.

These were clothes I would wear if money wasn't an object. The slacks were cropped to my shins, impressive since I was a shorty, and the top fit at my waist as if it had been tailored for my measurements. Even the shoes—a chunky gray heel that was comfy but added oomph and professionalism to the pants—were my size.

The food. The nap. The shower. Makeup and clothes. I felt pampered and confident. And I'd wear that like armor until my insides matched my outsides.

"You're such a badass, Simone."

Saying it out loud boosted the sensation even more. I grabbed the keys Brianne had left for me and headed back downstairs, refreshed and ready.

CHAPTER FOUR

At the foot of the stairs, movement caught my eye. Stretched out in the lone patch of sun still peeking over the house was a patchwork cat with one ear missing. Its stick-thin, ratty tail wrapped itself around its haunches. His little claws were painted a bright shade of pink, and a fabulous bright blue bow adorned his neck.

"Gumbo!" At his name, the cat turned its head to survey me with two different colored eyes. I crouched down and extended one hand. "Hey, Kitty, remember me? Gosh I can't believe you're still around. You were old when I was a teenager!"

The cat sneezed, stood, and arched its back. Oops, I'd offended kitty.

"Aww, Gumbo, I'm so sorry if I offended you. You look fantastic. I'm just thrilled to see you alive." Gumbo watched me a second longer, then sauntered past me to the door to the wellness center. His tail brushed my leg which, for a cat, basically means you're their best friend for life. Score one for Simone.

I wasn't sure if Gumbo was allowed inside, but he walked straight in like he owned the place when I opened the door and turned right into a room I didn't remember seeing earlier in the day. I followed him into what seemed to be a conference room, He hopped into one of the large corporate chairs surrounding a long, rectangular table.

"This must be the board room." I moved to sit next to Gumbo, who was perched as if he were waiting for the meeting to start. Gumbo let out a quick hiss, glared at the head chair, then glared at me.

Huh. Gumbo was right. Technically, I was in charge now. I should sit at the head of the table. But would the people I'd never met before take it the wrong way? It was bad enough they suddenly had a new owner they'd never met. How would they feel about the power play?

"Meow." Gumbo didn't meow. Not exactly. Instead, it was like he said the word meow in a slightly high-pitched and effeminate voice.

"You're right, Gumbo. It's my seat."

I'd no sooner settled myself in the seat than Brianne sauntered in carrying a stack of booklets. She stopped short when she saw me, and I regretted my chair choice. Yes, I was at the head of the table, but it was the head closest to the door. I had to swivel and crane my neck to greet everyone who walked in.

Not exactly commanding.

"You're here. Ooh, and you look great. I love that top on you! I trust you're feeling better?" Brianne went over to the drink table that rested under the window on the far side of the room and returned with a fresh glass of ice water. "Unless you want caffeine?"

"No, actually, I don't want to be jittery when I meet everyone." And I'd just been thinking I needed water. How could she have known that? "Thanks. You know, if you show me around, I'm happy to get my own drinks. I don't want you to feel like you have to wait on me or anything."

"I don't mind. I enjoy taking care of people." Her smile told me she meant it. "Wait to read that. Hiya, Gumbo, love the bow." She tapped a finger on the spiral-bound booklet she'd set in front of me, then set one in front of each of the chairs, including the cat's. Gumbo peered at the paper, his eyes moving like he was reading it.

Which was odd, not just because a cat looked like it was reading, but because the papers were all blank. I flipped through each of the pages, angling them to see if the light picked up invisible ink or something. But no. Brianne was passing out binders of blank papers.

And things were about to get weirder.

Ethan's deep chuckle floated down the hallway before he made it to the room. On his arm was a woman I recognized right away. Tall and slender, with an athletic tank and leggings, both in a bold blue accenting her impressive muscle tone. Her platinum blond hair was pulled into a high ponytail, and eyes bluer than her clothes lifted as she smiled adoringly at Ethan.

Lauren Whitaker.

The head cheerleader in high school. Ethan's girlfriend from freshman year through graduation. And a holy terror of a bully who'd belittled and mocked anyone not in the popular group. Including me.

I took a sip of my water to try to steel my nerves and ended up clanging the glass against my teeth because I was too busy looking at the girl I'd wanted to be instead of the thing in front of my face. I sputtered, water dribbling down my cheek, which is when they turned their attention to me.

"Simone, good to see you again. I trust you're settling in upstairs?" Ethan took my hand in both of his, swallowing it up. He was warm and soothing. "You clean up well." His thumb stroked my wrist for a hot second, and I do mean hot. Then he released my hand and stepped back. "Do you remember Lauren Whitaker from high school? She's the head physical therapist here at Magnolia."

"Of course I remember Lauren." I extended the same hand—still tingling from Ethan's light caress—to shake hers. She may have been awful to me, but I could be polite. Especially if they were still together and Ethan's slight flirting had been all in my head. But hadn't he said he was divorced? "How have you been?"

"Fantastic, Simone. And it's so good to see you." It was weird, but the way she shook my hand wasn't fake or forced. And her smile was genuinely friendly, if a bit apologetic. "When Ethan told me you were returning to Treater's Way, I immediately whipped out my yearbook to get the visual. You're even prettier now than I remembered."

The laugh escaped me before I could stop it. It's not that I wasn't pretty in high school, but standing next to a supermodel when you feel like you belong under a bridge is disconcerting enough. To have her tell you that you're pretty is a step too far outside reality for my own tastes.

Her eyes widened with shock, and Ethan suddenly found his fingernails very interesting. But before I could apologize, Lauren's hand was on my forearm.

"That's a fair response. I'll be the first to tell you, I wasn't the nicest person in high school. I'm certain I owe you an apology." She dropped her voice to a whisper. "Back then, I was going through a lot. I took it out on others, rather than face it myself."

My heart gave a little twang at the tremor in her words. I knew that kind of pain, even if I didn't know the specifics.

"We all get better with age, don't we, Lauren?" I patted her hand.

"We're like fine wine. Or so I've heard. I only drink the cheap stuff myself."

My throat constricted, like it did when I said something I didn't mean. I thought back through my words. I didn't think I'd gotten particularly better with age, and what I'd said to her felt more like a platitude than a genuine sentiment. I couldn't remember any specifics from our past, though. Had she done anything more than ignore me, spread rumors about me, and talk down to me? My reaction felt too strong for run-of-the-mill bullying.

There was something else. A hazy event just on the edges of my memory. She'd been the jealous sort; I remembered that much. Possessive of Ethan and his time, and he'd kept our morning workouts a secret even though they were innocent. That was, until ...

Until, what? I couldn't find the details anywhere in my mess of a brain. She released my arm with a grateful smile, looking relieved and comfortable. Did I trust that she really thought she wasn't nice in high school? Did I believe her apology would be sincere?

Or was I projecting emotions onto her because the last time I was this close to a woman who looked like her, she was in my bed with my husband, and I threw up on her shoes? Yeah, it was probably that.

All things I could analyze later, when I was alone and less overwhelmed. For now, since Ethan had said Lauren was a division head and therefore on this mysterious board, it was time to make small talk.

"So, you two stayed together, huh? That's fantastic. The stats on high school sweethearts remaining married were definitely against your odds."

"Actually, we divorced right after college." Ethan pulled a chair out for Lauren, then took the chair between us. "But we've remained pretty close. There's no animosity. We just wanted different things out of life."

"Like marriage." Lauren jabbed Ethan's side, and it was such a sibling-like gesture I had to smile with them. "Ethan wanted to collect them, and I didn't even want one."

"And you did fine without it." Ethan opened his phone and slid it across the table for me to see. It was a shot of Lauren, smiling proudly, snow and sky flying around her bright orange jacket.

"Holy cow, is that Mount Everest?" I swiped through a few of the images. Yeah. She'd climbed a mountain.

"I can't believe you keep these on your phone." Lauren retrieved the image and smiled at it like a doting mother. “Was that the second time or the third?”

“I can’t keep track.” Ethan grinned at Lauren’s stuck-out tongue. “This was the one where you didn’t use your—”

“The Twins will be here momentarily. They were just finishing up a dual service.” Brianne’s brow furrowed as she nudged herself between Ethan and Lauren, taking his phone and locking it before handing it back to him.

“Who are the Twins?” I asked.

Brianne circled the table and took the chair across from me, absently stroking Gumbo between the ears as she directed her gaze to Ethan. I knew that look. I’d given it to my husband. It was a *don’t stick your foot in your mouth* kind of stare.

He’d been about to say something, and she’d interrupted on purpose. Huh.

“Lydia and Lyra, the medspa and salon division heads. We can’t start without them. Ethan, while we’re waiting, perhaps you can explain more to Simone about what was left to her? She was taken aback when I showed her upstairs earlier today.”

“Yeah, sorry about that, Simone. You were ...” Ethan stared at his hands again, and this time I let myself laugh.

“Not in a good place?” Ethan pressed his lips thin and nodded. Poor guy, he didn’t like uncomfortable situations. Which would be hard for him, because I tended to be awkward and create them.

Oh well, I may as well make it all the way weird.

“Lauren, just to fill you in, because I don’t know how fast gossip in this place travels, I caught my husband of twenty years having an affair with his physical therapist. I’ve been living in my office for the past week, trying to figure out what the heck to do about my screwed up life.”

Both Brianne and Ethan shifted their gaze to me, and the weight of the pity in their eyes was nearly suffocating. My chest already felt like I was wearing a corset, and my heart was pounding a thousand miles a minute. Having to bear people I’d just met feeling this sorry for me was too a step too far.

“I’m sorry, Simone. That’s disgusting of him. And unprofessional of her.” Lauren hissed under her breath, muttering a curse I’d never heard before. “Not that it makes a difference about what he did, but do you have kids?”

"One. A boy." The pressure bore down harder. "My son Gabe is studying graphic design in California."

They all stared at me, waiting for me to say more. Even Gumbo had his cute little head cocked to one side, the space where his missing ear should be angled toward me as if to hear me better.

I wasn't going to tell them more about Gabe. Not yet.

Plus, I only had thirty days to decide if I was going to stay and let these people get to know me better. And I was, at the very least, Brianne's boss and Lauren's business partner. I didn't understand fully, but it sounded like Ethan had more information to share with me. The last thing I wanted was their pity.

And I was tired of wallowing under it myself.

"I'll be okay, guys. I'm tougher than I look." As soon as I said it, my throat cleared and some of the tightness in my heart dissipated. That was usually a sign I believed what I was saying. Well, that was good to know. "I promise, you don't have to feel sorry for me. Let's get this board meeting started, already!"

They instantly sat up straighter. Ethan opened his mouth as if to say something, and Lauren fiddled with her blank pieces of paper. Then, somewhere in the house, a clock began to chime.

I'd not seen a clock or heard any other hour be announced. Each chime echoed like a gong, rattling our water glasses and sending picture frames on the wall askew. It was loud, but not in a way that hurt my ears or felt unbearable. The chimes had an otherworldly tone to them, a sound I couldn't quite place but knew I'd heard before.

With each bong, something inside me shifted, like a power rising to the surface. My toes and fingers tingled with it, and a vibration rolled up my arms and legs, centering in my stomach. For just a moment, I thought I'd lifted off my chair.

My world tilted sideways. The room swirled with magic. Which I would have believed was a ridiculous notion.

Until the Twins entered the room.

Because they were definitely not human.

CHAPTER FIVE

Ethereal beauty. That is what sprang to mind. They were a foot shorter than me, which was pretty unusual given my height. But their presence commanded attention. Their slight build reminded me of billowing wisps of grass, and they seemed to flow rather than walk into the room.

They barely cast a glance my way, greeting both Ethan and Lauren with warm hugs. One of them, her hair like metallic green mint, waggled her fingers toward Gumbo. The other tucked a strand of her long lavender locks behind ears that ended in a slight tip.

They glowed. Not just in a healthy skin or internal beauty kind of way. They literally glowed. The chairs at the tables pulled back to allow each of them to sit. Once they'd settled in, the chairs moved forward and closer together, as if they couldn't be separated.

Then they turned to me and spoke simultaneously.

"You must be Simone."

My mouth hung open. I lifted my hand to snap it shut, only to have it fall open again. I was having a stroke. This was a stroke or a nervous breakdown or ... something. Something was wrong with me.

They rolled eyes the color of an orange creamsicle dipped in satin and pursed their perfect, full lips. They turned to Brianne. She murmured something to them. They nodded in unison, then one of them spoke.

"Lydia Langley, Division Head for Magnolia Medspa." Lydia lifted manicured eyebrows the same gentle purple as her hair. She crossed her arms and placed both hands on the pages in front of her.

"Lyra Langley, Division Head for Magnolia Salon." Lyra's fingernails matched the mint of her hair. She repeated the crossed-arm gesture.

"Lauren Whitaker, Division Head for Magnolia Physical Therapy." Lauren cast an unsure smile in my direction. Then she, too, crossed her arms and placed both hands on the stack of blank pages in front of her.

I'd always been a fan of roller coasters. Until now. My stomach was rising to meet my throat, but my body seemed to be sinking into the ground at a hundred miles per hour. I didn't want to look around for fear I'd vomit, but out of the corner of my eyes, the walls appeared warped and shifted like funhouse mirrors.

I had no words. My mouth hung open like I was waiting on a momma bird to feed me. As I gaped around the table, the rest of the room continued the process, each time crossing arms then placing both hands on their booklets.

"Ethan Mosely, Lawyer pro tem for Magnolia Therapy and Wellness."

"Brianne Steele, Operations Manager for Magnolia Therapy and Wellness."

Gumbo's giant blue bow had twirled around to land on his chest. He was on his back, playfully batting at it with his painted claws. Brianne cleared her throat, and he sat upright, curling his tail around his body.

"Gumbo, Ancient Archiver and Mystical Protector of Magnolia Therapy and Wellness."

Gumbo's voice didn't sound ancient. He sounded like an adorably precocious little boy. Had he said ... Pawtector?

He was a living representation of an *I Can Haz* kitten. Exactly what I'd picture the voice of a cat being if they could talk.

Which, of course, they couldn't. Except Gumbo just had. He crossed his paws over the papers before him.

I squeaked. I literally squeaked. It was the only sound that would come out of my mouth. My heart pounded in my ears. My vision tunneled until only the table in front of me, and the five occupants and one talking cat, were visible. The rest of the room fell away. If I'd turned my head, I would see nothing but stars and space and sky.

A bubble beyond time and space enclosed us.

This was what dying felt like. I died in my sleep yesterday. Or that headache last week had actually been a stroke, and I'd passed into the great beyond. It was all a horrible nightmare. It was all a fantastical dream.

I wanted to ask. I couldn't ask. No words would form, and six pairs of eyes watched me, waiting with the expectation that I knew what to do. I opened my mouth to ask questions, to scream, to expel the buildup of pressure causing intense pain that radiated through my throat and down my neck.

Only one sentence came out, and I hadn't expected to say it.

"Simone Bardot, Acting Division Head for Magnolia Mental Health and Ephemeral Supreme of Magnolia Therapy and Wellness."

I didn't even know what ephemeral meant. As if on autopilot, I crossed my hands and placed them on the spiral in front of me.

Though it seemed like the entire process took several minutes, it had all happened before the clock reached the final gong. And as the clock struck six, the space around me cleared. We were sitting at a table again, with all but one chair filled. Brianne and I at the heads, Lauren and Ethan on the right, Gumbo and the Twins on the left.

And the booklet in front of me was no longer blank. Letters printed in a deep green ink floated to the surface.

Magnolia Therapy and Wellness
Monthly Board Meeting

My throat immediately cleared once I'd said the words. I followed suit with everyone else and opened the binder to the first page. It was titled **Second Quarter Recap**. I recognized some of the words from my own business accounting. Profit and loss. Annual projections. Blah blah blah.

Brianne read over them. Occasionally, Lydia or Lyra interjected but for the most part they all nodded and appeared to be following along. I turned the page when they did, feeling like I was in some sort of fever dream. Twilight Zone music played in my head.

"The Magnolia Medspa exceeded projected growth beyond the first quarter." Lydia's voice reminded me of birds chirping a morning song. Her statements rose and fell like they were lyrics in a poem. As she spoke, she gave me a crooked grin. My stomach danced. She could have asked me to pull my last hundred dollars out of my wallet, and I would have offered it to her on one knee. "The Mardi Gras recovery treatments were a big hit. Our goal will be to maintain that growth and ensure that at least seventy percent of the new clientele the packages brought in become repeat customers."

Her smile broadened and her eyes held mine.

"Don't you think that's a good number, Simone?" Oh, boy. The way she said my name. I could have purred.

Everything was so topsy-turvy. Ethan and Lauren were shifting uncomfortably in their chairs. Was I supposed to say something? I thought back on what she'd said, something about packages and clients.

Right. Customers. Because this was a business, and I was supposed to own it. I shook my head to clear the fog. It didn't work.

"How—?" I licked my lips and took a sip of water. "How do you plan to do that? Maintain seventy percent, I mean? Is that a reasonable expectation?"

There. I'd said logical-type words. Go me. Her lips pursed, the slightest deepening of her brow line telling me I'd not behaved the way she expected.

"I know," she whispered to her sister, who I was pretty sure hadn't said anything. "We offer beyond excellent customer service. And Lyra and I discussed throwing in surprise complimentary offerings. For example, if they were given a gift certificate and used it for a Mane Blowout, we'd throw in a Claws and Cuticles Manicure while I had them in the chair."

"That was my idea." If Lydia's voice was birdsong, Lyra's was the melody of every beautiful instrument playing the harmony of the universe at once. It didn't so much fill the room as it did create the very particles of air I was breathing. My heart fluttered. It literally fluttered like I was a teenager. "A large portion of the Valentine's packages were to the local werewolf pack's fated mates. As soon as summer warmed their fur, they redeemed them. And they tip well."

"I love it. It's beautiful and perfect." I heard myself say it, but I wasn't really there. I was floating in an otherworld where talking about fated mates and manes made sense. Something rushed through the air to tickle me, and I giggled.

"April is traditionally slow when Mardi Gras falls in March. A surprising number of the supernatural practice Lent. But Mother's Day was strong, and we began summer treatments in June, so my projections for the quarter held." She looked my way again, her voice brusque and lovely. "The projections for Q3 are there for you to read. I anticipate a drop now that word has gotten around that we are ... in flux."

"I don't think we'll be in flux for very long." Brianne nodded at me. "If we drop at all, I expect we'll rebound quickly."

Deep down, I got the sense that Brianne was complimenting me, or maybe encouraging me. The sneer on Lydia's face told me she didn't have the same faith. But I didn't care. As long as she kept talking.

Instead, she leaned back, and Lyra leaned forward.

"We ran out of purple and green body dyes after Mardi Gras. Plenty of gold, though." There was shared laughter around the table for the joke I didn't get. Lyra fluttered her eyes at me as she spoke. I giggled in return. Why the hell was I giggling so much?

"I've requisitioned more from the druids. They say House isn't cooperating. That it doesn't have the energy to grow what they need. Or won't." Her expression shifted as she glared at me. I'd let her down. I had no idea how, but the sadness of it punched me like a fist to the stomach.

"I'm sorry," I heard myself say. Did she say druids? And that the house wasn't cooperating? Some of it was getting through, like an insistent alarm interrupting a happy dream. But I just wanted to float.

"Don't be. You've done nothing wrong." Lauren's voice was unexpectedly sharp, and she was shooting angry glances at the Twins. Why would she do that? They were so sweet and lovely.

"We have time." Lyra made a dismissive gesture toward Lauren. "I shifted to pushing summer colors."

"Like your lovely skin." I smiled at Lyra. My voice sounded weird to my ears, sort of muffled and slurring like I was drunk.

"Ladies, that's enough." Brianne's glare cut through my haze. Whoa. She had the kind of glare powerful men can only hope to achieve. The Twins grinned innocently, lifting waifish shoulders to their ears. They waved their hands toward me.

Once they lowered their hands, a jolt of electricity shot through me, planting my butt firmly in the seat. I braced myself with the edge of the table. My head tilted backwards, and the dancing butterflies in my stomach suddenly coiled into a tight ball. A wave of nausea rolled through me. I trembled all over.

Swallowing water down, I fought the urge to vomit. Again. I no longer wanted to giggle, that was for sure. Embarrassment bloomed in my core. I'd been a fool, for reasons I couldn't understand, and the meeting was only halfway finished.

So much for a good first impression.

CHAPTER SIX

"What just happened?"

"I'm sorry, Simone." Brianne was at my side, though I hadn't seen her get up. She shoved a plate of cookies in front of me. "The sugar will help. The Twins don't always have respect for our Board Meetings."

Lydia and Lyra managed to look sheepish, almost wilting under Brianne's mom voice. I lifted a cookie, breaking it in parts and shoving a small piece in my mouth. Nothing made sense. Not the shifts in my sensations or the casual talk about dying fur and druids. I wanted to believe Agatha had been treating mass delusions when she died, and they were all a part of it, except I'd have to question my own eyes.

"We were just testing the waters." Lydia's formerly lilting voice held an edge of defensiveness. "She's supposed to be able to fight it."

My throat closed over the cookie I'd been fighting down. A sort of righteous anger burned inside me. My stomach soured with it. What was I supposed to be able to fight? Magic? Spells? I didn't even know they existed until twenty minutes ago.

Looking at the Twins now, they were still lovely, but the glow was gone. Their features appeared sharper to me, and the colored skin seemed faded. Just two more mean girls, magical or not.

Everyone was staring at me. I wanted to stick up for myself. I wanted to reassure them that Agatha knew what she was doing when she left everything to me. But how could I do that? I didn't believe it myself.

Whatever was going on, I was on the precipice of my entire world being upside down. Again.

They had doubts about me. I could understand that. But messing with me in a professional setting was a cruel way to express them. Did I have authority over them now? I thought back to the words I'd been compelled to say at the start of the meeting: Ephemeral Supreme.

I may not have known ephemeral, but I knew supreme. It was the leader of a witches' coven.

The thought tightened the knot in my throat. Did they believe I was a witch? Were they witches? Was this a coven?

I hovered in this state of believing everything I'd seen and none of it, all the while a table full of people and one empty chair sat and waited. And yes, I believed the chair was waiting for me to respond. As if it could read my thoughts, it gave a little jiggle.

My throat clogged deeper. My mouth was drier than the desert. I took a sip of water, hoping to release the pressure building within me. It didn't work. I'd just have to trust my words. I took a deep breath.

"I don't understand what is happening. I'm not sure if I'm awake or alive or what." I turned my attention to the Twins. "I'm pretty sure you two can snap me like a twig without even breaking your nails."

Their smiles grew sly, telling me I was correct about that. Yikes.

"What I can say is that we're all in unfamiliar territory here. None of you know me or know who I am, beyond some girl from high school who hasn't been to Treater's Way in thirty years."

I took another sip. Whatever was coming up seemed like too much for me to handle. I couldn't swallow it down, nor could I bring it to the surface. I kept rambling.

"I grew up here, though. My mother ran this place the whole of my childhood. So I must know something, right? Surely, I couldn't have been raised here and not seen, um"—I gestured around—"this before?" I turned to Ethan. "Right?"

Ethan shifted in his chair and glared at his fingernails. For an aggressive lawyer, he really didn't like confrontation. Same, dude. It was Lauren who spoke for him.

"What do you remember, Simone? Anything?"

"Honestly, it's all a distant memory." The clock I hadn't seen gonged, and my ears buzzed. A flash of something ran through my mind. Water and trees. A small park bench. Me, a hair over eighteen, crying until I was empty inside. Boiling rage. An uttered oath.

But as I tried to grab the memory, the rage simmered, and the image faded. The clock gonged again, and Brianne shifted in her chair.

"I'm sorry, but we really must continue the meeting. Can we move on for now, Simone?"

Her voice was tight. I didn't understand why continuing the board meeting was such a big deal. I mean, in general, meetings were a lot of saying stuff that could be handled in an email anyway. But she was one of the only people actually making me feel welcomed here, and I didn't want to add to her stress.

"Yeah, sure, in one minute. My point is that I'm going to need all of you to show me grace. And patience. I'm not going to strut in here power-hungry and change everything. I just want time to understand what the hell is going on. Agatha gave me thirty days. Can y'all give me that as well?"

"You got it, Simone." Gumbo, who I'd already forgotten could freaking talk, hopped onto the table and rubbed his head against my shoulder. His cute kitten voice and loud purr put me at ease. He sauntered back to his seat, but when the chime happened again, he cast a nervous glance at the empty chair. It wriggled closer to the table, so I pointed at it.

"Who's sitting there?"

"We'll discuss it after the board meeting." Ethan gestured toward Lauren. "For now, can we continue?"

Why did they keep asking me? They'd started the meeting without me, hadn't they? I was mostly sitting there with my big dumb mouth hanging open.

"Simone?" Brianne had returned to her chair. She reached across to the space in front of the empty table and patted it, as if a hand were there. She'd placed a spiral notebook there as well. Huh. "We need your words to continue the meeting."

"Oh." Well, that was interesting. I looked down at my own packet. I'd forgotten where we were. This was why I hated meetings. "Lauren, it looks like you're next." I gave her my best *I'm a professional and not at all on the verge of a nervous breakdown* smile. "Please continue the meeting."

"Right, thank you, Simone." Her return smile held an approval that soothed a bit of my nerve. This was definitely not the bully queen bee from high school. Maybe she really was on my side. I wanted to believe that. But then again, a physical therapist had just screwed my husband, and even if I didn't want to be *that person*, part of me unfairly held that against Lauren.

Oops. She was talking about important business things that I should have been paying attention to.

"... but we'll see how they feel about that in August. Y'all know how difficult trolls can be."

There was a collective chuckle of appreciation around the table. I smiled like I was totally in on the joke.

"In other news, the charmed injury recovery treatments are showing promise on our test clients. There are some muscles we can't get into with dry needling or cupping, even with enchanted equipment. The fae in particular have deeper aches and bruises." She winked at Lydia and Lyra, who let out twin titters.

"Thankfully everyone in Illusion Square has recovered from The Battle, and they are rebuilding. I heard someone is opening a craft store on one of the top floors. We've got a strong community because of them, and lots of opportunities for town growth."

"What's Illusion Square?" I felt bad interrupting the flow of the meeting, again, but it felt important that I know.

"It's the shopping center that surrounds the Mighty Oak at town center. Ana built it to feed our tourism industry." Lauren paused to see if I was following. We had a tourism industry in Treater's Way? Huh. "Do you remember her, Simone? She was the librarian when we were kids."

"Vaguely," I said. Like most things about the town, it was a distant memory. Still, the name Ana brought a warm feeling to the pit of my stomach, like she was someone safe. I needed to explore the town when I was less overwhelmed. Maybe it would spark some familiarity. Then again, what other surprise magic would I find if I revisited my past?

They were all watching me, waiting again, so I waved a hand at Lauren. "Thanks. Go ahead."

They all turned the page, and I followed suit. A fresh new horror engulfed me when I realized I would be expected to talk about the Magnolia Mental Health Division. I barely heard the rest of Lauren's talk. What would I say? My heart pounded in my head.

I'd been on this soil for all of four hours. I'd spent several of those asleep. Now I was supposed to give a report about a company I barely knew?

A company that, I was beginning to see, was much more than it appeared on the surface. Apparently, it catered to werewolves and fae and who knew what else. Which begged the question ... what kind of clientele could I expect?

Was I going to become a therapist for the supernatural?

What issues could the supernatural have? Would I be counseling vegetarian zombies or narcissist vampires?

Oh, God. Lauren was done. It was my turn.

What had Agatha been thinking? I couldn't run a company. I had no idea how to run an entire organization, let alone a single division. I'd driven my own practice into the ground. Hell, I hadn't even had a cup of water to offer Ethan when he visited.

I was spiraling. Big time. And they all sat and waited while I did it.

I glared at Ethan. This was his fault. He hadn't prepared me for any of this. Even taking out the supernatural element, he hadn't been clear about what I'd inherited. The walls were closing in on me. I was struggling to breathe. I couldn't do this. I wasn't even sure I believed any of it existed.

I opened my mouth to speak, just to fill the silence, hoping words would magically form. "I don't ..."

The empty chair beside Lauren lifted off the floor, halting whatever nonsense I was about to spout. It lifted over the air and hovered over the table, twirling until it faced me. I was staring at an empty chair, but it didn't *feel* empty. I squinted my eyes at the chair, barely able to make out the shape of a female. As I strained, she came into sharper focus.

Long, stringy gray hair. Harsh lines on a wise face.

"Agatha."

Her eyes warmed and she smiled at me. It was funny how seeing her brought more of her memory into focus. It had been Agatha who'd encouraged me to become a therapist. Who had consoled me when my mother died and looked after me until I finished high school.

Who'd understood when I had to leave and supported me. Right before I'd left, she'd told me something.

I couldn't remember what she'd said. It was right there for me, but I couldn't grab it.

Whatever it was, it felt important. Agatha had always believed in me. That was why she'd left me her business.

I had to believe in myself or at least fake it until I did. I had literally nothing to lose.

I took a deep breath, centering myself, willing my shoulders to soften. As if she knew I was getting it, she gave me an encouraging nod. The chair returned to its place, still empty. No one looked at it, so I wasn't sure if I was the only one who'd seen her. Even so, the interaction with her, even if it was in my head, calmed me.

This wasn't a hardship. This was an opportunity. My whole life had been pulled out from under me just last week. I'd caught my husband with his hands in the cookie jar. I'd gotten into an argument with my son and said words he may never forgive me for. I'd retreated to an empty office and the practice I'd barely mustered the energy to maintain.

I didn't want to go back there. Sure, I didn't understand what was going on here. Not fully. And I had more questions than answers. But one thing was certain. I sure as heck wanted to know more. So, I let my voice guide me.

"First, my condolences to each of you on the loss of Agatha. My memories of her are distant, but I remember her empathy and kindness. Even when she was staunchly set in her ways."

Small chuckles echoed through the room.

"I assume Agatha has left case files for me?" I waited for the dual nods from Ethan and Brianne. "So, I'll be reviewing those before I start to see clients. I also need to familiarize myself with the town, which seems to have changed a lot in thirty years. And I want to understand our business better."

I swallowed a few times, letting the clog in my throat relax as I found my words.

"I didn't know the supernatural existed. Part of me still thinks maybe I'm having a stroke or lucid dream. I have a lot to learn. And only thirty days to do it."

The chair rumbled again, all four legs lifting and slamming back to the floor.

"I get the feeling a whisper of Agatha is still holding on, probably until she believes I can confidently operate as both a division head and, um, a Supreme." I let my eyes land on the Twins at the end of my statement. Though their faces were expressionless, Lyra lifted one eyebrow. "What I will say is that, if I'm going to do this, I'm going to have to do it my way."

I was just as surprised by the words that had come out as the table. Lydia cracked the smallest of smiles. Standing on my own two feet would win their respect. And though my default core desire was to please others, that hadn't exactly been working for me as of late. So, I just let myself continue talking without overthinking.

Apparently, my voice knew it was time to make waves.

And my voice was the only thing I had, so I may as well trust it.

"I can't speak to the second quarter earnings. I'm going to defer to Ethan who likely received instruction from Agatha about the meeting. I'm going to absorb as much as I can, and give myself permission to let it all settle in. Then, we'll move forward, and I assure you I'll either be ready for our next board meeting"—I closed the report in front of me—"or not here anymore."

I stood up, my legs barely holding me in place. I had to get out of here. I needed to find a place to breathe and process.

"This may or may not be my place, but I'm adjourning this meeting."

I didn't give them time to argue or correct me. I turned tail and ran out of the boardroom, trusting my feet to take me somewhere safe.

I should have known where I was headed.

CHAPTER SEVEN

The world wasn't actually closing in on me, but it may as well have been. My vision tunneled to just a blurry view of the streets around me. I walked, then I ran, until I reached my destination—unsurprised to find I knew the way despite all I'd forgotten about my hometown.

When I reached the graveyard, I leaned against the cool granite of my family mausoleum. My fingers traced my mother's name while I fought for breath. Someone had been taking care of it. Fresh daisies, my mother's favorite, grew in lush patches.

I wanted to hold onto sensations as long as possible. The smell of freshly mowed grass. The cool damp of freshly watered soil sinking into my fancy new slacks. The unexpected laughter from a family far in the distance.

I needed something to root me in place. But my stomach jumped and tumbled and flipped all around like the contents of a dryer. My heart pounded so hard I put my hand over it to still the fabric, as if it might beat straight out of my chest. I fought for breath. Tears stung my eyes.

As far as panic attacks went, this one was a doozy.

Anytime I was even the slightest bit upset, the same two damn things always happened. My throat would close until I could barely swallow. Then I'd throw up. I dug my fingers into the grass. Something was rising from deep within me, and it was going to force its way to the top no matter how hard I fought.

Maybe I should have let it surface. Maybe it would have freed me from all this upheaval. But the woman I was at forty-eight didn't have the common sense that my eighteen-year-old self had. Or the emotional anchor of another person to pull me back from the edge.

When I was young, my mother had been a pro at talking me down from panic attacks. They'd happened almost daily after she died, and Agatha had taken over for her. In college, I learned a dozen tools to help my clients when they were lost in emotion. Still, the basic technique from my childhood was still the most effective.

I reached into the dregs of my memories to find their voices, buried deep.

Something about senses. I squeezed my eyes shut, then opened them wide.

First, name five things I can see. A magic house. A magic town. Fresh daisies. Purple people. A talking cat.

Next, name four things I can touch. A shirt altered to my body. Pants that fit my short legs. The cold stone of my mother's burial site. The tears on my cheeks.

I couldn't think straight. Three things I could hear? Wasn't that next?

The rush of blood in my ears. A whimpering sound that apparently came from me. A bird chirping overhead as if it had any right to be so damn cheerful.

I let out a frustrated grunt, shocking the laughing family. They mumbled something to one another, then walked away, leaving me alone.

Except I wasn't alone. The hair on the back of my neck stood on end. A wake of chills blanketed my skin. I was being watched.

I hauled myself up, brushing dirt off my pants and peered around the corner of the mausoleum. Squinting, I could just make it out.

A dog. But if it was a dog, it was a massive one. It was like a wolf. A wolf that, even crouching behind a gravestone, could not hide how tall it was. Its eyes bore into me. They were familiar enough that I debated taking a step forward, which was testament to just how far gone I was.

Sure, Simone. Walk toward the not-at-all-native animal that looks like it could eat you with one bite.

"Fancy a pet, CC?" I let out a squeak as Gumbo weaved his lanky frame around my legs. "You still get panic attacks?"

I glanced down at Gumbo, then back to where the wolf stood seconds earlier. There was nothing there.

"I think I'm hallucinating." I plopped down to the earth. "I think I'm broken, Gumbo."

"You're going to be fine. I can help." Gumbo rubbed his tail against me, his adorable little voice lightening my mood. I closed my eyes and enjoyed the moment while my thoughts ricocheted around my head like a manic ping-pong ball. "Pet the kitty whose fur is softer than silk."

The cat talked me down. A talking cat talked me down from a panic attack. Sure.

Gradually, while Gumbo reassured me, my emotional tunnel widened, and my chest opened. His purr was like a vibration that connected me to the universe, giving me a feeling of being rooted in place that I hadn't realized I longed for. My stomach settled, though I wished I had a soda or something to absorb the acid. Something cool and wet cupped my palm. A glass of ginger ale, packed in ice.

"Did you do that?"

"Did I do what?" Gumbo's bow and nails were now a bright lime green.

"This." I waved my glass. "What happened to your ear?"

"A battle. Long ago." Gumbo's words were a slur. He adjusted again and curled onto my lap, tucking his tail and paws underneath like a talking, furry potato, his eyes on the glass in my hand. "You must have done that. House is too tired."

I replayed the past few moments in my head. I didn't remember saying I wanted a soda out loud. Of all the strange things that had happened, though, a mystical soda seemed the least important. "House?"

"It only has so much energy these days, and the board meeting ran long. That's not completely your fault. The Twins' shenanigans didn't help matters." For a moment, the cute kitten facade faded, and his voice was rough and angry. "I knew they would toy with you. Irksome fools.

"With their mayhem, your questions, and holding two Supremes in one space, the meeting took more power than usual. House doesn't exactly have it in spades right now." His innocent kitty voice was back. He stretched his paws, circled again, then settled with his head resting on my knee.

"Two Supremes?"

"I'm sure Ethan will explain it all tomorrow." Gumbo closed his eyes.

"I'd sure like you to give me some answers today." I rested my head against the stone. I didn't want to wait until tomorrow for answers, especially when they would only lead to more questions. "Even a little bit of information will help me sleep tonight."

"As you wish." Gumbo leveled a glare at me, hopping off my legs to sit and face me. "Agatha's spirit fractured when she died. Part of it went with her body, to ensure passage to the beyond. The other part is acting as Ephemeral Supreme, until you embrace your role."

"What exactly does ephemeral mean?"

"Temporary." Gumbo let out what I think was a chuckle. "Agatha was ready to pass in the end. She's annoyed that part of her is still here." He rolled to one side, exposing his chubby cat belly. "But you weren't ready."

"That's probably my fault." I risked a belly rub, grateful he didn't attack my hand. You never know with cats.

"It's no one's fault, Simone. Things changed when your mother died, so Agatha gave you space. Perhaps more than she should have. You were supposed to return. Something happened that kept you away."

"What?" It teased the edges of my memory again. A park bench. Tears of rage and shame. A determination to leave. A pull to stay.

"Wish we knew." As if that settled everything, he returned to my lap. "We expected you twenty years ago."

My heart stuttered. Twenty years ago, I was pregnant. I'd considered leaving Jeff. We'd gotten married instead. Treater's Way had called to me even then, that much I remembered, but something kept it at bay, like a distant memory of a time when I was happier.

The only bright spot for me in the past twenty years had been my son, and in a fit of rage I'd damaged our relationship. Maybe irreparably. Bile burned at my throat.

"Jeff happened. Jeff kept me away." It wasn't entirely true, but it was close enough to feed the sick pool of betrayal still floating inside me. I could have built a life here, raising my son in the town where I grew up. Instead, I'd devoted myself to taking care of a man who couldn't even do laundry. "Wherever you are Jeff, I hope all your clothes stay dirty forever."

"Be careful, Simone." Gumbo's ear rippled. His eyes darted around.

"Why?" I swiveled my head. We were still alone, though it was getting dark. "What happened?"

"Your magic happened." Gumbo hopped off me with a sigh, giving up on his hope for a nap lap. "You're a witch, you know. Your words have power."

"Huh?" My magic? I have magic?" I'd just begun to grasp that magic was real and apparently surrounded me. The idea that I had magic of my own was a step too far.

"Agatha chose you for a reason. A supreme is an extremely powerful witch." Gumbo lifted one paw to clean between his toe beans. "Given the magic you wield when you speak out of instinct, I'd say you're a word witch."

"What's that? I can say spells or something?"

"Eventually. You have a natural ability to understand different languages, and words probably come easy to you in difficult situations. A word witch usually has a power center in her throat, and it's connected to her heart. So you recognize emotions, and they rise so you can speak them."

Well, he was partially right. I did have a gift for other languages, and I definitely could read emotions. Whenever I felt my own, it was like a physical sensation in my heart and throat. But words coming easily in difficult situations?

"That doesn't sound like me."

"If you say so." I hadn't realized cats could sound so sarcastic. "If I'm right, and I usually am, your words have the power to soothe and the power to command if you let them. It's a benefit to your patients, I suspect."

"I definitely haven't been beneficial to my patients. At least not lately. Actually, I've barely had any patients. One in the past week. A strange case that led to a headache and heartache."

"What about before that?" The way Gumbo was watching me, I had the sense that I was missing something obvious. But try as I might, I couldn't figure out what it was.

Had I ever been a good therapist? I liked to think so. In college, and during my clinicals, I'd exceeded above and beyond my peers. It had even led to a shiny corporate job that paid boatloads of money and slowly sapped the life out of me.

Of course, I'd lost it a few years later when my son was born. But even my private clinic had thrived early on. Hadn't it? It felt like a million lifetimes ago.

"I don't know," I finally answered. I didn't know, and I was too exhausted and overwhelmed to think about it further. "But we should get back to the house. It's getting late, and I thought I saw a dog earlier."

"A dog?" The fur on Gumbo's rat-like tail fluffed up. I couldn't help but laugh. This cute little mystical protector was scared of dogs.

"Or a wolf? I can't be sure. But don't worry." I scooped him into my arms, holding him close for a quick cuddle, then carried him all the way home as night settled around us. "I'll protect you, buddy."

CHAPTER EIGHT

I had already decided I didn't want to meet with Ethan in the boardroom before I received his text suggesting we meet upstairs so we could chat privately. I'd managed to stumble to the bedroom the night before and grab a solid ten hours of rest.

In the light of morning, I looked at the house with fresh eyes. I'd thought someone had gone through the effort to guess my tastes and decorate for me. But more than one of the division heads had referred to this space as House, like it had its own personality. Or magic.

"Good morning, House. Thank you for making me feel so welcome." A surge of joy pushed through me, like a child receiving praise for cleaning their room. There was an air of familiarity in here I hadn't noticed before.

I was starting to put some puzzle pieces together. For some reason, I'd forgotten most of what I knew about Treater's Way when I left for college. There was a crucial memory clawing at the back of my mind, eager to come out, but it felt blocked. And, given that everything surprised me and yet somehow felt familiar, I suspected magic was the culprit.

"I'm looking forward to getting to know you again." A wave of nostalgia warmed my chest. Apparently, the house felt the same.

Something clattered in the kitchen. When I went to investigate, I found a charming drink nook in the corner by the breakfast table. I didn't remember it from the day before. Maybe it wasn't there.

Fresh coffee gurgled from a full pot, its inviting aroma making my stomach grumble in return. A small tray of pastries sat on a pretty, pink plate. At the center were two large, blueberry muffins. I lifted one, warm in my palm, and took a bite.

There was something about food, eaten at the right times or in the right way, that sparked emotions. I could never be one of those people who viewed it strictly as fuel. A fresh aroma. A tart berry on your tongue. The lift of your mouth when you chewed.

It's like it sends you back in time or cements a moment inside you.

"I used to bring these to Ethan, didn't I? After our morning workouts, we'd sit on the bleachers and chat and eat a blueberry muffin." Looking back, we'd been better friends than I realized. But we'd kept it a secret.

Maybe Ethan could tell me why.

The breakfast corner overlooked the back garden. When Ethan arrived, we settled there. I cracked a window to let in a soft breeze, thanking the house for providing it. It was mid-July, but this was the temperature other parts of the country must refer to as spring. As much as I loved Louisiana, it wasn't because of the weather.

"You look better this morning." Ethan's eyes lit up at the muffin I passed him from across the table. We ate in silence for a few moments, enjoying the birds chirping and the dim laughter that lifted its way up from the Wellness Center.

"It's funny." Ethan toyed with the mug of coffee I hadn't noticed appear in front of him. "Growing up, I always wanted a reason to come here. Back then it was just the therapy center. When I was fourteen, I begged my dad to bring me with him. He was Agatha's lawyer for years. He let me, and one of these delicious muffins popped onto a counter for me."

He took a big bite, making exaggerated "mmm" sounds as he chewed.

"After that, you brought me one once a week when I'd see you on the track."

"Thank the house, not me." I shoved the last of my muffin into my mouth, washing it down with the most perfect cup of coffee I'd ever had. "I know I dropped my mom here for work before school, and the bag would be waiting for me on her desk. I can't tell you if I knew how it got there or not."

I let comfortable silence hang between us. I had so many questions, but part of me wasn't ready to start asking. I needed to take my time. Ethan, for his part, seemed content to wait.

"Can we start with the easy stuff?"

Ethan chuckled, wiping his mouth on a napkin and laying it over his plate.

"I'm not sure there is easy stuff."

"That's fair." I took a breath. "Why did we keep our friendship a secret when we were in school together?"

"You remember that?" A flicker of pain passed through his eyes.

"The muffin brought it back," I said, gesturing at my crumbs.

"That's not an easy answer." Ethan took a sip of his coffee, then grimaced as if it were suddenly bitter.

"Was it Lauren?"

"Only partly. It was also ..." Ethan's voice trailed, and he shifted in his chair. "You really don't remember why?"

I closed my eyes, trying to peer behind the curtain that shielded me from the past. The breakfast, and my talk with Gumbo, had it cracked. It would take a lot of effort to pull it all the way back. I wasn't sure I wanted to.

"It was Ray, wasn't it?" Just saying his name was like stabbing myself in the heart with Cupid's rusted arrow. A brief fling senior year should not hurt this bad. But it had sent me running, and Ethan was part of that. Nope, I definitely didn't want to go there yet. "Okay, new question. What does mental health have to do with pedicures?"

"That sounds like the start of a very bad joke."

"Or a good one," I said. We laughed together, and with each snicker, my shoulders softened, and my jaw loosened. It really was like picking up with an old friend. When your old friend grew up insanely hot. "You have to admit, it is an odd combination."

"I can see where you're coming from. It was Lauren's idea." Ethan's smile shined with pride. "She brought it to Agatha fresh out of college. She'd been treating a particularly difficult client and suggested he might benefit from therapy."

"That's clever." I took our plates and returned them to the sink, mumbling a quick thanks to the house. "There's often trauma associated with injuries or physical pain. Releasing that can ease the recovery process on both fronts."

"That's exactly it." Ethan chuckled and shook his head. "Once Lauren discovered she was a witch, there was no stopping her."

"Lauren's a witch?" I paused midway to my chair, my mouth dropping open. The Twins were fae, and Lauren was a witch. Allegedly, so was I. Maybe this really was a coven.

"Well ... yeah. The Center runs on magic." He twitched his eyebrows. I didn't think I'd missed something obvious, but apparently I was being dense. "Lauren has natural healing abilities. She combines that with modern techniques to treat a clientele that wouldn't otherwise be able to seek relief."

"When did she learn she could ... do that?" The Lauren I remembered from high school had not been so selfless.

"Senior year. But the years leading up to it, when her power was building but she didn't understand why, were tough for her." Ethan pressed his lips firm, as if he regretted saying anything. "That's her story to tell."

I decided to let that subject drop. He was right, it was Lauren's story to tell. I was a different person in high school, too. Given the Twins' response to me, it would be nice to have another ally in the house. Maybe I should let go of what I did remember from thirty years ago and shape a new path forward. Maybe if I did, the parts I couldn't remember would come back to me.

"Okay, let's get to business." I waved my hand like I was waving away the space between us and sat down. "What do I need to know about the next thirty days?"

"Right." Ethan pulled a tablet out of his briefcase and opened it on the table, rotating it and scooching closer so we could review it together. "You have thirty days from yesterday's board meeting to establish your place as rightful Supreme and Division Head. Brianne is the manager, and she can help you learn the ropes and answer most of your questions about the day-to-day. And the other division heads are required to support you." He wrinkled his nose. "Even the Twins."

"What happens if I don't do it?" A sudden dryness coated my throat. "What happens if I can't, or don't want to, establish myself?"

Ethan swiped the screen, scanned it, then closed it and tucked it away.

"Let's not worry about that just yet. I'm sure you're going to do fine."

Whoa. That was a heavy tone for something that was supposed to be placating.

"Didn't Agatha have family? Anyone other than me she trusted?" A glass of ice water appeared on a coaster on the table. I gulped it down. I still felt like I was swallowing sand. "Why can't Brianne become Supreme?"

"She had a distant family that is not under consideration." Ethan's tone was sharp, making me wonder about this "distant family" he wasn't going to expand on. "Brianne is mundane."

"Brianne?" I barked out a laugh. "She's anything but mundane."

"No, I mean she doesn't hold magic. She can support the Supreme, but she can't become one." Ethan fidgeted in his chair. "Do you mind if I pace?"

At my nod, he stood and walked, his long stride eating the small space between the kitchen and breakfast nook. I'd already figured out that, despite his big tough attorney facade, Ethan struggled with uncomfortable situations. And so far, every situation we'd had together was uncomfortable. I waited, letting him process how much he wanted to say to me. It seemed easier than asking a ton of questions. I didn't want to pry answers out of him, but I would if he didn't give them willingly.

Finally, he stopped and sat back at the table, angling his chair to face me fully and leaning forward.

"Okay, here's what I know. This is the second version of Agatha's will. Well, technically it's the third, but no one ever saw the first one. What we refer to as the original copy was created by my dad the year we were born." He paused for effect, and probably to make sure what he was saying sank in. "The year your mother started her job here."

My gut vibrated. It was a new sensation. I was so used to getting nauseous when I was processing or upset. But this was different. This was deeper than a stomach issue, as if my roots were waking up from a long nap.

"Are you saying she added my mom to her will?"

"No." Ethan tugged on one of his curls. It was kind of adorable how exasperated I could make him. "She added *you* to her will, Simone. From the moment you were born, she expected you to become Supreme."

Wow. No pressure there. The vibration was growing. My body was trying to tell me something. I dug my nails into my palms, trying to focus on whatever it was. What did I know—what was I forgetting?

"I think …" I paused, swallowed, and tried again. "I think I knew that. I was always going to come back here." The vibration echoed in my throat. Yes, that was what I needed to say. "It's all fuzzy. My life happened, different from how I expected it to go. But deep down there's something here."

I waved my hand over my stomach, then past my chest to my neck.

"An inner voice whispering that I was supposed to return sooner." I blew out a breath. "I don't know what to say."

"Agatha warded you away. She told me about it when we met to revise the will last week." She said you two had an agreement. You went to college, finished your clinicals, and got some experience. Then you were supposed to return here twenty years ago to train under Agatha. You didn't. She assumed the ward held, keeping you from returning, though she didn't know why."

He sat back with a sigh and shrugged his shoulders.

Last night, Gumbo had told me something similar. I'd blamed Jeff. But after a night of sleep and calmer emotions, it wasn't fair to place it all on him. I'd chosen to stay. I hadn't wanted to return to Treater's Way or face the pain I felt when I thought about home.

We sat in silence, Ethan watching me process in much the same way as I'd watched him pace earlier. We knew each other well, which still baffled me. Then, a realization hit home.

"Did you say she changed her will last week?"

"I did." Ethan grinned, as if he'd been waiting for me to catch up. "Right before she died, she called me here to make one small change. A thirty-day observation period."

I groaned. The chair in the boardroom, Gumbo's comment about part of her still here.

"I'm being judged."

"Agatha doesn't judge, Simone." Ethan took a moment to rest his hand on my forearm, giving it an affectionate but brief squeeze. "She would say she assesses."

I had to smile. From what I remembered, that sounded like her.

It was all so overwhelming. Every time I started to process one piece of it, another piece popped up. I was incomplete and blocked, and it was frustrating.

“Why did she make the change last week?”

“Surely you know why?” Ethan canted his head, and I lifted my shoulders to my ears. Was I always going to feel like I didn’t know things I should? “Because of the meeting you two had.”

“Meeting? I haven’t seen Agatha in thirty years ...”

My voice trailed, and two things happened at once. A blinding headache shot through me, stabbing me behind the eyes like a thousand needles. And my stomach twisted into a giant knot that refused to release its grip. I ran from the table, knocking my chair over on my way to the sink, where I lost every bite of that delicious blueberry muffin.

It didn’t taste as good coming back up. I retched until I was empty, dipping my head under the faucet for relief. Then I sank to the floor, water puddling around me.

Last week, a strange woman had rushed into my office seeking emergency counseling. It was a bizarre session that, under normal circumstances, I would have remembered more clearly. I’d made notes on her session. Immediately after, a blinding headache prompted me to leave my office and return home.

Which is when I’d found Jeff in bed with another woman.

“The woman that visited my office last week was Agatha?” My throat was swollen and tender. “It didn’t look like her. Or what I remember of her. It was the strangest session of my life.”

“Why?” Ethan handed me a towel and sat on the floor opposite me. “Can you tell me what it was about?”

“I suppose it’s relevant.” I opened my phone, scrolling to my notes file and pulling up the last session. Scanning it, a million little puzzle pieces fell into place. “Patient is suffering from anxiety due to her certainty that she will die at midnight. She requested assistance determining who to leave her estate to.

“I’d humored her, in a way, walking through scenarios with her using a tool called the miracle question.” I slid my phone toward Ethan, allowing him to read the rest. “Her favorite option was the one where she hung on for thirty days to make sure she felt confident in her choices.”

CHAPTER NINE

I didn't need Ethan's suggestion that I take a few days to process before diving in to know it was a good idea. My head was swimming. Given what little I knew about witchcraft, and with a bit of feedback from Gumbo, it seemed like Agatha had used a glamor. The woman who'd rushed into my office one week prior was definitely not the Agatha I'd known.

She'd been more poised, with flame-red hair and piercing eyes and perfect makeup. And, despite her stress at the situation, she'd been remarkably in control of her emotions. I wanted to read through my notes from the session and try to reconcile them with my lapsing memories, but not yet.

As comfortable as the house was, my body longed for movement. I wanted fresh air and to tour the town. It irritated me that there were so many barricades in my head. It was my hope that a jog around Treater's Way might shake them loose.

Well, not a literal jog. I hadn't gone running in years, and though I missed it, I didn't think starting a new exercise regimen at this moment would be a good idea. Although, if I were a soon-to-be divorcee, wasn't that exactly what I was supposed to do? I went through the mental checklist of things my patients had done once fresh off a divorce. I'd already cut my hair, but I could dye it a different color or get super fit. Or get a tattoo.

As if he knew I was thinking of the D-word again, my phone

exploded with texts from Jeff. I scanned through them, rolling my eyes at the increased use of caps. He'd started off with gentle words and an insistence that it wasn't what it looked like. He'd actually tried to convince me he'd been getting a therapeutic massage. You know, the kind where both people end up naked.

Now that over a week had passed and he wasn't hearing from me, his texts were getting more aggressive.

Why haven't you come home??

I went by your office, it's EMPTY!

Simone, YOU'RE being RIDICULOUS!

STOP BEHAVING LIKE A CHILD, WOMAN!!!

I really loved it when he called me "woman." I was in no rush to speak to him. As far as I was concerned, he didn't need to know anything about this new opportunity. He'd only try to talk me out of staying, and though I hadn't made up my mind about anything, I wanted the choice to be mine.

In fact, the more I thought about it, the more I felt like I'd spent too much time reacting to everything the world threw at me. I was an adult, with a voice of my own and damn good instincts when I chose to listen to them. I didn't need Jeff, Ethan, Agatha, or anyone else for that matter telling me what to do.

Maybe it was time I found my own voice.

My phone dinged again, setting my last nerve on fire. He couldn't even bother with a phone call?

"I hope you get blisters on those text-loving thumbs of yours, and they never heal." Gumbo's warning about my words echoed in my mind as I laced up my shoes. I firmed my lips and shoved my phone in my pocket.

With a few more steps, I arrived at the small house where I'd grown up. Someone had painted it stone blue, a huge step up from the drab gray we'd had. There were whimsical curtains in the windows, and a wind chime tinkled softly in the summer breeze. Mom and I had a lot of love, but not a lot of money. It was nice to see that, whoever lived there now, was taking good care of the place.

I followed the sound of excited laughter around the corner. In the fenced-in backyard, an adorable little boy chased a fat gray Labrador. The boy's bright blond hair was glued to his face with sweat, and red circles lined his chubby cheeks. He climbed on the back of the dog, whose head was bigger than the boy's entire body. Together, they raced around the small patch of yard.

Unexpected tears welled behind my eyes. As annoyed as I was with Jeff, my son Gabe was caught in the middle. He'd been joyful and chubby like this once, too. And at only twenty, he still needed his mother. I hadn't been there for him, and I'd totally screwed up our relationship. It was a knife in my heart to think about.

The boy and his dog had grown silent. They'd stopped playing to stare at me from the far corner of their yard. The dog tilted its massive head, reminding me of Cerberus. I smiled and waved at them both. The dog grinned back, his tongue lolled out, and a full cup of drool fell to the ground.

"Hi!" The boy shouted. "We're going to race!"

"Good luck!" I called back, then wandered away. I wasn't sure if anyone in this neighborhood had been around thirty years ago, or if they would remember me. A woman staring at a young boy was just a little too creepy for my tastes.

As their joyous sounds faded, it occurred to me the dog could have actually been Cerberus, tempting me to go back and look harder for a second and third head. Come to it, the boy could have been a wizard or werewolf or something. Who knew?

Then again, I'd been human when I was growing up. Mundane, I corrected myself, then stopped.

Except I hadn't been mundane. I'd been a witch the whole time and didn't even know it. Had my mom known?

Treater's Way was a walking town. Few cars passed by, and my feet found their way to my old high school without any help from my spiraling mind. Growing up, it had always struck me as odd that some of the top minds in the world clamored to teach in a small town like this. The building itself was state of the art, and even thirty years later it still gleamed like new. Treater's Way High had one of the highest education ratings in the United States, far above the rest of Louisiana. I was beginning to understand why that was.

My memories of high school, and even my youth, were a patchwork quilt containing bits and pieces of events. I'd been a bit of a loner in my day, with only the occasional friend. I'd kept to myself, aside from my morning runs with Ethan. Despite how incredibly hot he was today, we'd had nothing more than a friendly flirt back then. There was a boy named Alex I vaguely remembered. Lauren and her hive ruled the roost. But had I had good friends or felt like I belonged?

No. Not until I'd met Ray Chase. Him, I would never forget.

Even now, the thought of him crept through me like a predator. Ray Chase, high school quarterback and immensely popular, despite his bad boy attitude. Long and lanky and solid muscle. With arms that made a girl purr.

I swallowed several times, trying to coat my mouth, which had suddenly gone dry. I'd never been on his radar until senior year. He'd been injured in a game, and I was mourning my mother's sudden death. We'd found comfort in each other. The hottest summer of my life.

The way I'd cared for him had cemented my plans. Helping him recover, mentally and emotionally from the devastation of that injury, pushed me to become a therapist. Agatha had always guided me in that direction, but Ray gave me confidence in my ability to make it real.

The dry mouth disappeared, replaced by a bitter coating that only Ray could bring to me. He'd left me so abruptly it sent me reeling. Armed with a scholarship and nonstop tears, I'd left Treater's Way, swearing that ...

Swearing that what? It was there, on the edges of my memory, not yet ready to do anything but taunt me. I'd reached Illusion Square, the area Lauren had explained was now the bolstering hub of the town.

Good timing. I needed a coffee and to leave memory lane.

CHAPTER TEN

I don't know what I'd expected, but this trendy shopping center was an absolute marvel. The Mighty Oak, a massive tree with branches so thick and spread so wide it was a wonder it could hold itself up, acted as a centerpiece for the square. I wandered closer, nodding at the frazzle-haired woman murmuring to herself at its base.

But the nearer I got to the tree, the more I understood it was not a normal tree. Thirty years ago, this area was nothing more than a dirt-filled make-out spot, so I'd never had a reason to visit. But now, I could sense the vibrations that shot down from every leaf and rumbled through the roots.

"This is the heart of all of our magic." I clasped my hand over my mouth, shocked to find I'd uttered the words aloud. The massive branches rustled their approval.

"Darn tootin' she is." The woman, in her sixties but with an air of youth to her that made me feel younger just being in her presence, giggled. She resumed her whispering, and it was then I realized she was talking to the tree, not herself.

Only a week ago, I might have questioned that. But now everything was different, whether I wanted it to be or not. Now, I found myself wondering what it was saying back to her.

Bistro tables and park benches surrounded the tree, and they were packed despite the heat. The shops themselves were four different buildings, each with two floors. I read the signs for each building, smiling at how unique and yet simultaneously homogenous it all was.

An apothecary displayed rows of bottles and soaps, the comforting aroma of which mingled in the air around me. An art store boasted beautiful canvases and supplies. I wasn't much of an artist, but it gave the impression that anyone who stepped foot in there could find their inner Rembrandt. A sign in the glass-enclosed display window announced a new craft store coming soon upstairs.

I wasn't very crafty, either.

At the far back was a gardening center with vibrant pots and leafy plants that I'd surely kill if I brought them home. Peeking out from the forest at the back was a wooden bridge, sparking a memory. What was across that bridge?

I considered exploring further, but the coffee shop to my right drew my attention. A crisp and welcoming breeze pushed my back, and I ventured forward. Inside, Brianne nursed a thick mug, eyeing it like a long-lost lover.

I hesitated, unsure if I should interrupt her moment of passion, when her eyes lifted and bore into mine.

"Hey, girl! Come on over and join me."

"I should order first."

"No need. Ms. Ana will be along, and she likely already knows what you want."

I took the seat she motioned to with a grateful smile. There was no menu on the table, but as I turned to read the board behind the cashier stand, a familiar figure approached me.

"Hey, Ms. Ana." I did that awkward thing where I didn't know whether to hug or shake her hand. I rose halfway, only partially surprised to find she already had a drink and was reaching it out to me. "It's so lovely to see you again."

I didn't ask if she remembered me. It was clear from her expression that she did. And I'd already given up on questioning it.

"Simone Bardot, my goodness you've aged gracefully!" She closed the gap between us, setting the drink on the table and pulling me into a motherly embrace.

I held on longer than I'd intended. It had been a long time since I felt comforted this way. It shook up all the tumultuous pieces inside me, waking up a longing for affection and support that I'd buried deep when Jeff fell ill.

No, a tiny voice whispered inside me, I'd buried it long before that. Granted, we'd never been incredibly passionate. But when did my comfortable marriage with Jeff become two roommates who happened to share the same bed?

Whether I wanted to believe it or not, that happened long before his affair.

"Welcome home, dear." Ana's smile was patient and warm, as if she knew a single hug had sent me into turmoil. "I expect you're settling in at the Magnolia?"

"Trying to." I attempted a shrug, but my lips trembled. As a kid, when I wasn't working out or hanging with my mom at the office, I was at the public library. Ana might have been the coolest librarian ever. She had a matronly air, but everything about her was as vibrant and youthful as the town itself. Like things aged here without getting old.

"Aww, hon, give yourself time. It's a lot to take in." I didn't question how she knew what I was going through. I knew enough about small towns to know that one person's business was everyone's business. When Agatha died, I'm sure the rumor mill went crazy trying to find out who took control of the Magnolia. "You know, when everything around you feels uncertain, the best thing you can do is find an anchor."

"An anchor?" I let her guide me back to my seat next to Brianne.

"Yes, dear. Something to root you in place. To help you feel secure and less adrift. You know, like a good friend." She gave Brianne a quick side embrace and me a final warm smile. "Enjoy your day, you two."

"Well, that was subtle." I chuckled along with Brianne, taking a sip of my drink. Then, my world stopped. Tiny squeals of delight danced through my taste buds. I was floating on a caffeinated cloud of happiness. "Oh. My. God."

The moan that escaped me was straight up erotic. Brianne's head tilted back, and she laughed like she hadn't in years.

"Oh my." She wiped tears from the corners of her eyes. "I forgot how everyone responds to their first drink here."

"What is it?" I was a little lightheaded.

"It's different for everybody." Brianne tipped her own mug so I could see the caramel-colored liquid inside, different from the dark frothy drink that had washed all the bitterness from my mouth. "Ms. Ana has a knack for knowing what people need."

"I dimly recall it being the same when she was a librarian. Good to see she still knows books." The coffee shop was divided in two. On the far side were rows of weathered bookshelves and inviting recliners, a few of which were occupied by people lost in their own worlds. "Maybe that's her magic. I wonder what she is."

I glanced back at Brianne, who was gazing at me as if trying to solve a puzzle, making me wonder what I'd said. Was that offensive, to ask what kind of magical creature someone was? I didn't know the rules. Besides, wasn't Brianne mundane? God, I hated that term.

My throat tightened, and I fought to find something to say to correct the situation. Brianne was the most welcoming person I'd found here, and we were starting to become friends. I didn't want to screw it up by shoving my foot in my mouth. Ana was right. I needed an anchor. Finally, I settled on being honest.

"I'm sorry if I offended you. I'm learning to adapt in a new world here." I took another sip of my drink, but it didn't have the giddy effect from earlier. With just a few words, I'd managed to make myself feel small and out of place. Again.

"Would you like to come to my house for dinner Friday evening?" Brianne smiled at me and patted my arm. It was a domestic and welcoming response. Man, she was good.

I agreed to go, and we chatted about normal things while we finished our drinks. But the feeling that I was handling all this wrong stayed with me. I knew I'd be up all night, questioning every turn of phrase I'd used.

It was like I couldn't relax into a single moment, even a benign one, without my inner voice nagging at me. What was wrong with having a friendly coffee with someone I liked and respected? And why did I feel like, if I didn't do and say everything completely perfectly, I was failing at life?

If I were one of my patients, I'd issue a diagnosis and begin treatment. I've never been particularly good at treating myself. Even when, logically, I could see where my thoughts differed from reality, the ability to gain control of myself seemed to elude me.

"I want to turn it all around so badly." The words were a blurt I hadn't expected, interrupting Brianne's idle chatter about a bed and breakfast on Bridge Island, whatever that was. “Sorry,” I said when she once more tilted her head to inspect me. “I didn’t mean to interrupt.”

“You can, you know. Turn it all around, not interrupt me. You just have to find your voice.” Brianne stood to leave, and I rose with her, taking our cups to the nearby cleanup counter and waving goodbye to Ana. “Good thing you don’t have to do it alone.”

“I’m sorry I’m so awkward.” I walked Brianne to the edge of Illusion Square and hugged her goodbye.

“Sweet Simone, you’re so hard on yourself. Stop all that negative self-talk!” She squeezed me tight, then released me, holding onto both of my hands. “Ana is right, you need an anchor. Guess it’s gonna be me.”

Crap, there were the tears again. I’d been so starved for support and friendship. Now it was being offered to me in abundance, and I was struggling to accept it.

“You want some advice?” Brianne dropped my hands and fished for a tissue from her purse.

“Sure,” I answered. “Hit me with it.”

“I know you’re struggling to believe this, but Agatha chose you because she knew you were capable. So dig deep, friend, and find a place to start chipping away at that massive wall of self-doubt you’ve built.”

After another quick hug, Brianne strolled off, and I turned to take another look at the Mighty Oak. It was a beautiful tree, but it was no ordinary tree. I was positive there was magic in it, all the way down to its roots. Maybe beyond.

I didn’t know my roots, not really. My father was never around, and my mother never talked about him. She’d been isolated from her family. Still, we’d been a close-knit duo, and with Agatha’s support, we’d had a happy life.

I’d been happy here once. I had a second chance to be happy here again. The question was, how did I start? The tree shook its tallest branch, making me feel smaller than ever. But it didn’t feel like it was judging me. I trotted over to the base. The older woman from earlier had gone, and I was able to see the concrete pool that surrounded its roots. A compass rose was etched into the center. The water rippled, and a shadow off one of the branches pointed behind me, in the direction of the Magnolia.

“I get it,” I said to the tree. Now I was the crazy one talking to trees. “It all starts there.”

As I headed back to the Magnolia, I wondered what I would find there to help me. Gumbo was asleep in the window when I opened the door. He opened one annoyed eye then resumed his nap.

I headed into the living room, contemplating my own nap on that pretty, red couch. But several boxes of files rested on the table in front of it. I skimmed the first one, and a spark of hope cut through my tiny critical voice.

Once upon a time, I'd been a really good therapist. Before my practice had died, before I'd given up and gone on autopilot, before my husband's sudden and terrifying illness. I reminded myself of that as I reviewed the files Agatha left me.

This was where I'd find the confidence I lacked. One client at a time. Propping my feet up, I leaned back and dove in.

CHAPTER ELEVEN

First thing Monday morning, I headed downstairs to see my first clients at Magnolia Therapy. Brianne guided me to one of the large wooden doors in the main entryway, opening it to a massive office on the other side. There was a stale, musty odor to the room, like it sat unused for years.

Given that the house seemed to prefer order and cleanliness, that struck me as a bit odd. I'd assumed no one had been in this room since Agatha's death, but it felt like no one had stepped foot in here for years.

Unlike the upstairs, it wasn't redecorated to my tastes. But it didn't feel like Agatha, either. The waiting area was clinical and dated, with floor-to-ceiling dark wooden bookshelves and straight-backed chairs with no cushions. No one would be comfortable sitting here waiting for their session.

The floors were the same shade as the bookshelves. There were no windows to let in sunlight. No rugs or vases of flowers to create warmth or soothe a nervous soul. From my review of the notes, I knew already that Agatha and I had very different clinical methods. But this room was unforgivably depressing.

In my mind, I pictured an ideal waiting room. No need for a reception desk, since Brianne was outside. Two thick, cozy chairs that allowed a couple to sit near each other without having to snuggle close. I'd want them in bright, soft shades of green and pink, sort of like sitting in a garden. And a fuzzy white carpet to offset the dark of the wood.

No patient was going to read the clinical reference guides that currently overflowed from the bookcase. But I wouldn't want them to have fiction either, as most patients tended to hide from their issues. There were books I recommended to patients all the time. Nonfiction parenting guides or marriage tips. And some personal items to make it feel less cold and more homey.

On a whim, I'd purchased a plant in Illusion Square over the weekend. With no natural sunlight, there was little chance of it surviving. But I could bring it down with me in the mornings, perhaps let it sunbathe over the weekends. My thumb was as brown as they came, but surely even I could handle one evergreen.

The therapy room itself was worse. More bookshelves. More stodgy books. A long brown leather couch sparked a memory of Agatha's faux-visit to me. She'd taken one look around my office, lifted her eyebrows in disapproval, and inquired where my couch was. Even after I'd explained I preferred modern methods of therapy to the traditional couch-based practice, her lips had thinned with judgment. Of course, now that made sense.

At the far end of the tiny room was the biggest, heaviest looking desk I'd ever seen. It was polished to a shine, with chunky legs and brass drawer fittings. It was so deep that someone sitting on the other end would feel a thousand miles away from me. The chair was the same shade of brown as the couch. Nothing about it invited me to sit there for hours listening to others.

Yuck.

I couldn't remove the couch right away. Agatha's patients would be used to it, and I didn't want to shock them with too much change all at once. Especially now that I knew how different our methods were.

My modern, solutions-focused practice would jar her patients, who according to her notes had been seeking therapy regularly for fifty or sixty years. How would they respond to my desire to get them actively out of their own way, rather than just letting them talk through their pain ad nauseam?

I wondered again why Agatha had chosen me. Even if she'd planned for me to take over in my youth, surely her visit before her death would have changed her mind? Surely she would have chosen someone more like herself, someone who met her approval, before she passed.

Although, of course, she hadn't had time. I was her last resort. The only one with a *Walk-Ins Welcome* sign and no one in the waiting room.

I winced as I plopped into the oversized chair behind her desk. My desk, now. It was hard and cold and unforgiving. I rubbed my sore tailbone, not even bothering to fight the sense of frustration welling up. Defeating thoughts raced through my mind.

You didn't do anything to deserve this. You're not a good therapist. The road ahead is too jagged.

And that's where I stopped the thoughts. Closing my eyes, I went to one of my favorite techniques. Pretend magic is real, Simone. I snorted at the thought.

If you awoke one morning and a miracle happened, the core of your problem was completely erased, how would you feel? I sat up straighter in my chair, a strange itching sensation dancing across my arms.

It was the very method I'd offered Agatha. The wording haunted me with its familiarity. *Let's say a miracle happened ...*

The memory danced forward, then flitted away again before I could grab it. As it left me, intrusive thoughts returned. And, because I always made my patients do it, I confronted my thoughts out loud.

"Simone, a miracle has happened. You are now the benefactor of a thriving practice in a charming small town. All of your dreams are coming true. How do you feel?"

I swiveled in my chair, as if addressing myself.

"Excellent question, Simone. I feel hopeful and nervous. Thankfully, I know I can rely on my training to help me gain confidence. I'll review who my patients are, identify their core issues, and assess how I can best help them learn to help themselves. I want to empower them, and to honor the memory of my benefactor."

I swiveled again, taking on the therapist role, hoping no one came in and saw me having a full-on conversation with myself.

"Great answer, Simone. You've reviewed your patients' files and will see your first one soon. In the meantime, what one thing can you do to propel yourself forward?"

I closed my eyes, visualizing my office and waiting room. Even if I only made it through the first thirty days, the space could use an update. Checking my watch, I had time to talk to Brianne about ordering furniture and decorations.

I pushed away from my desk and headed toward the main lobby. I never made it out of the waiting area.

It was the room I'd envisioned in my head. My plant was nestled into a new window that overlooked the backyard, bathing the room in sunlight. Comfy chairs angled toward the light. A huge white fuzzy carpet softened the space.

Currently on it was Gumbo, his bow and nails the same shade of sunset orange.

"Oh, this is soft." His baby voice vibrated with his purrs, like a tiny toy engine being revved as he kneaded the rug. "This might be my new favorite room in the house."

"Did I do this?" How many times would I stand under the weight of utter surreality? Would I ever get used to magical redecorations? Or was this what it meant to be a word witch? I touched the fabric of one of the angled chairs in wonder. "Can I speak anything into existence?"

"Did you describe this out loud?" Gumbo hopped onto the chair and turned in a circle, curling his tail around him.

"No, I just thought about it." I turned in a circle to take it in. "I pictured it in my head."

"And House took it from there," Gumbo replied. "To some degree, it can manipulate time and space. Everything you envisioned exists in stores somewhere. They'll have a record of it shipping."

"Cool." Cool was an understatement, but it was all I could manage. Looking around, I realized this *was* a magazine-perfect waiting room. I'd seen it in a magazine a few months ago, flipping through the pages on a long day with no patients. I'd allowed myself a moment to dream about the perfect office. The same office I'd envisioned moments earlier in my office.

"What does the therapy room look like?" Gumbo opened one eye to view the door, then yawned. "I'll check it out later."

"It won't be different yet. I can't see it." But I would. "House, can you store all of the stuff that was in here before somewhere safe? So that, if this doesn't work out, you can restore it? Whoever replaces me may have different taste."

I didn't know if the house could hear me, but I figured it was worth a try. There was a sense of agreement, as if the house understood. Underneath that understanding was a second presence. The fractured Agatha, no doubt, looking on from the great beyond with pursed lips and folded arms.

"Replaces you?" Gumbo tilted his cute little head. "That's not how this works, Simone."

He closed his eyes, shutting off any further questions. It sat like lead in my stomach. But I could be nervous about that later. My first supernatural patient was set to arrive.

CHAPTER TWELVE

My first supernatural client turned out to be human. Mostly.

I'd read Doug Holloway's folder through three times by the time he arrived. It was a hefty case, both because Agatha took notes that rivaled the details in a violent epic fantasy and because Doug had been a patient for a long time.

Twenty years long.

Talk therapy was the oldest and most reliable method. It was also ineffective. Agatha had been a huge fan of letting a patient lie down and tell her about their mother. And sure, it had its place, I knew enough about Doug to get a visual of him before he entered.

But it didn't give the patient, even a supernatural one, any power.

Despite the magical element to my practice, I had to believe that the same fundamentals I would use on a human patient applied. The problem was, I wasn't sure how Agatha's patients were going to react to my methods.

Doug wasn't her longest-term client, but he was up there. After twenty years, Doug still had no agency in his recovery. He simply showed up and chatted. Our first session would be a good opportunity, for him and me, to decide if my new massive life change was permanent or not.

I was determined to make headway with Doug today. Maybe it was selfish, thinking of my own needs before the patient's, but I needed the win. After reading Doug's history, I had to believe he needed the win, too.

On a whim, I angled the couch and added the even-less-inviting chair Agatha had stashed in the corner. Too much change could increase a patient's anxiety, but I wanted to offer some options. Even if having options for myself made me nervous.

A small chime alerted me he was in the waiting room. I took a deep breath, both to release my own tension and to clear my personal space so I could be there for my patient, then opened the door.

"Doug Holloway? I'm Simone. Would you like to come in?"

I'd never applied the term resting bitch face to a man before. Deep wrinkles and bushy gray eyebrows only accented the appearance of a surly old guy. He wasn't that old, early sixties according to his file, but he *felt* older. He paused on his way into my office and surveyed the room.

"I decided the waiting room needed a spruce up." I gave Doug my best formal smile and gestured to the office. "Don't worry, not much has changed there."

His only response was a grunt. Not a good start. When he reached the doorway, he halted again, so quickly I almost bumped into him. I edged around his tall frame and followed his eyeline to the new position of the couch.

"Like I said, not *much* has changed." I smiled again, hoping I looked encouraging and not terrified. "You're welcome to choose the chair today or return to the couch if that's where you're most comfortable."

I was only half-surprised when Doug, after a moment of glaring at both, chose the chair. His slacks were almost chest high and starched to perfection. His shirt buttoned near to his throat with nary a wrinkle. Everything in the way he moved and the efficiency of his actions told me this was an ex-military man, even if I hadn't already read his file.

I took my seat, closing his folder in favor of my reliable yellow notepad and a comfy pen, and clasped my hands on the desk.

"So, Doug, I've had time to review the extensive notes that Agatha left. And I see you've been a patient of hers for a good long while. Since we've never met, and this is a lovely opportunity for us both to start fresh, why don't we take a moment to get to know each other?"

Doug's bushy eyebrows lifted a fraction of an inch, my only indication he'd heard me. My notes told me he'd transitioned from military to detective in Chicago until his forced early retirement due to an altercation with his partner.

My notes also told me he had a unique ability. And, given that I had the distinct impression I was being analyzed right down to my roots, I believed it.

"I'm going to confess to you that I'm nervous, Doug. Did you know you're my first patient in a very long time?" His eyebrows lifted a little higher. "Well, I had one other brief session. But this is the first scheduled one in quite a while."

Doug's lips thinned, but he didn't speak. He must have been an amazing cop.

"Doug, would you like to start by telling me about your gift?"

According to Agatha's file, Doug could read people's intentions at a glance. He'd know if I was lying, he would sense if I was nervous or unsteady, and he'd "see" any efforts to misdirect him. I needed to be completely honest or he'd never trust me.

He let out an annoyed grunt, prompting me to check his notes again. Dammit. I'd already misspoke. Even after a lifetime, Doug still struggled to embrace his magic. I wondered if I would feel the same way in fifty years then shoved the feeling aside to focus on my patient.

"Sorry, Doug. I shouldn't have referred to it as a gift."

"Worse gift than socks at Christmas." Doug's voice was sandpaper and gravel shaking in tupperware.

I chuckled at his statement, but his face remained deadpan. Okay, Simone, he hadn't been joking. Noted. I was going to have to take a different tactic here to open him up. Find common ground. Since I'd grown up here and he hadn't, it wouldn't be the town. Plus, I didn't remember half of it.

What did we have in common? Only one thing. Or one person. And just like that, the perfect memory sprang to mind.

"Every year at Christmas, Agatha knitted me a new present. It was always the same shade of blue, like she bought the yarn wholesale and needed to get rid of it. It was a pretty color, but never something I could actually use. Scarves. Hats. Tea cozies. She gave me a pot holder when I was six. My mother called them my Blue Hoard."

Doug's sudden laugh filled the room. It was a rich sound that lifted the tension from us both. A comfortable warmth settled in me. Not only had I found a way to reach him, but the thought of my mom and Agatha grounded me. I'd had a life here once. Maybe I could find it again.

"Okay, Doug." I put my pen on the desktop and folded my hands, giving him my full attention. "Would you like to tell me about your ability?"

"Not much to tell." Doug's shoulders lifted in a deep shrug. "If you're doing or saying something that goes against your nature, I know it."

"How?" I leaned forward a bit, conveying my interest. "In all of Agatha's notes, I noticed the detail of your magic isn't in there. Given that a week ago I didn't know anything like this existed, you'd be helping me out if you explained it to me."

"Thought you were here to help me?" Doug bit the words out, an edge of his frustration showing through. Good. He was taking the bait.

"I want to help you." I leaned back and smiled, gesturing at his massive folder. "It's difficult to do that from a stack of files, though."

Silence crowded the room as Doug's eyes met mine. A clock ticked on the far wall, a clock I hadn't seen earlier. At least the house had a sense of humor. I held firm, gnawing on the inside of my lip.

At long last, Doug grunted at me and waved his hands.

"You have a shadow. Sometimes it has color." He traced an outline of me. "When you aren't being true to yourself or you're telling a lie, it gets darker. Big lies go black."

"That must have been helpful when you were catching bad guys." His lips thinned again, and I realized I'd made another misstep. Why was I struggling with my words? "And even more difficult when someone you trust is being dishonest with you. Like your partner in the force, who was on the take and put your life in jeopardy for money."

His dark eyes flooded with unshed tears that surprised me. When was the last time Agatha had acknowledged that pain? He cleared his throat roughly and shifted in his seat.

"We all got hardships. Mine ain't so bad." His fingers fluttered to his collar, as if verifying he had it buttoned. "I'm only here because my wife makes me." The fingers clasped into a fist, exposing gnawed-on, dirty fingernails. "What I meant to say was, my wife made me."

"Your childhood sweetheart Maggie. Her death three years ago must have been devastating." I felt his pain all the way across the room, and it struck a chord I wasn't interested in plucking at the moment.

Jeff wasn't dead, but my husband was gone, too. Years from now, would I feel the pain of our breakup the way Doug did? We'd raised a child together. Would I mourn this loss forever?

I didn't think I would. I hated to admit it, but I barely missed him. My life was immensely different and yet, in terms of how often I saw or talked to him, it was the same. Maybe I hadn't realized how far apart we'd grown.

Or was it that I'd never loved him in the first place?

I pinched the soft flesh between my thumb and index finger. Just enough to bring me back to Doug and the moment. My rambling mind and insane empathy had their time and place. It wasn't now.

Something about Doug's case was resonating with me, though. Maybe because it was my first supernatural one. Or maybe because he struggled with his gift, and I'd never known I had one. At least not a magical one.

We'd been silent for three full minutes. While I waxed rhapsodic internally, Doug was staring out the window behind me. I tried to bring him out a bit more.

"Know what else Agatha wrote about your sessions? That you spent a lot of time staring at the ceiling and not talking."

"At least the window has a better view than the couch." Doug's dry smile broke my heart. The love he'd had for his wife sat on him like another skin.

He'd promised her he would seek therapy. He'd never intended to actually benefit from it. I couldn't blame him. Ray was from a generation where men didn't show feelings. They certainly didn't talk about them.

Which was why Agatha's well-meaning but outdated methodologies hadn't made a dent in his resolve.

But his pain enveloped him like a shroud. It was a shield he'd worn to keep the world at bay, dented only by his wife. Now she was gone, and he was stuck in a dark past with no hopes of living out the last years of his life, of which he should have plenty, with any sense of joy.

Since he still wasn't talking, I referred back to his notes. Doug had three grandchildren, still young. He had a job with Lone Wolf Sentries, a local security firm. He tended a garden in his backyard. He still had a life worth living.

Maybe I could help him see that. I took a deep breath and decided to use the tactic that had gotten me into this mess in the first place.

CHAPTER
THIRTEEN

"Doug, I'd like to try an experiment with you. Would you be willing to attempt something new today?"

It was almost physical, the barrier he put around himself. I waited, holding his eyes so he could read my intent and see it was pure. I didn't love being analyzed so thoroughly, but if it showed him I wanted to help, then I'd let it happen.

Finally, he lifted his chin an inch, which I took as an agreement.

"Let's imagine that tonight, while you are sleeping, a miracle will happen. The miracle is that, when you wake up, your pain and anger is completely gone."

His eyes flashed, a quick and violent jolt that literally pushed me backwards in my chair. I'd stumbled into bad wording. Again. What miracle would Doug actually want? Not to be free of the anger. To be back with his wife.

Damn, I should have acknowledged that.

"We can't bring your wife back, or escape our past, Doug. Even with miracles. Can you try envisioning a world without so much pain with me?"

His anger was only growing. A vein bulged on his neck, throbbing with each grind of his jaw. I kept going.

"Tomorrow morning, you're going to wake up and discover you can hold the memory of your wife without the painful guilty sensation that you pushed her away."

A flush rose along his cheeks. He was fighting me and fighting the session. But I needed him to see this would benefit him, so I kept pushing.

"This same miracle allows you to acknowledge that what happened with your partner was not your fault. That he took advantage of your trust for his own benefit. And that turning him in was the right choice to make because it protected the lives of your colleagues and innocent victims of his crimes."

His shoulders dropped, just a fraction of an inch. It was hard to tell if that was a sign of progress or not. For someone who could read others so well, he was damn hard to read himself.

"Do you believe that's possible, Doug? That you can feel completely valid and real emotions about the people you loved and trusted without the accompanying guilt that is also valid, but maybe not as real?"

"Can you do that, Simone?" Oof. Doug could cut to the core when he wanted. His ability was something else. Not only could he see the ebbs and flows of my emotions, but he could also sense the parts I was squashing down.

Or he'd heard about Jeff's betrayal in town. I wasn't in New Orleans anymore. Small towns knew everything about everyone. I had to allow for both possibilities.

"I don't know yet, Doug." There was no sense in being dishonest or evading the question like he had done. He would know. "I hope to one day."

Again, that sensation of being read like a book. He slumped in his chair, and a flicker of hope lit within me. I was making progress.

"So back to this miracle, Doug. When you wake up tomorrow morning, what will be the first sense that something is different?"

I'd used a version of the miracle question with Agatha when she'd come to my office. It was an effective tool for helping a client shift from problems to solutions. With Doug, I hoped it would help him see there was an end to this cycle of pain. If only he would grasp it.

Doug closed his eyes. As soon as he did, the feeling of being analyzed evaporated. If he was shutting other people's sense of self out, perhaps he was digging into his own.

"We slept in different beds." He opened his eyes briefly, a hint of humor lightening his features. "I snore."

As I matched his smile, he closed his eyes again.

"I always woke up before Maggie, so I'd put on a pot of coffee before I left for work." His voice caught, rough with the emotion bubbling to the surface. "I wanted her to start her day easy. And while I was at work, I'd picture her, sitting with a cup of the coffee I brewed for her, looking out at the garden we created together."

"That's a nice image. I'm sure it helped you get through the hardships of your job."

"I've been making that same damn pot of coffee every morning since she died." A tear streamed down his cheek. I wondered if he noticed it. "At the end of the day, the damn pot is still full."

When he opened his eyes, I knew I'd made a dent. It was as if he was lighter. Not a lot, but just enough.

"So what does tomorrow look like with this miracle, Ray?"

He took a deep breath, and I held mine.

"I don't make a full pot of coffee. I remember that nice thing I did for Maggie, and lord knows I was a hard man to love but she did, and I remember that I made her happy, too."

And the dent widened. It's temporary. I'd seen enough patients to know that this wasn't a permanent stick. But it allows them to see past the moment, to give themselves an ounce of hope. And they could use that hope to effect change.

"How would that affect the rest of your day?"

He was there, right on the edge of a minor breakthrough. I helped him in our very first session! I wasn't a shitty therapist after all.

"It would make me spend the day feeling like the ass who forgot about his wife." His face was hard again, and a huge scowl brought his eyebrows clean over his eyes.

I'd celebrated too soon. I should have known better. Resisting hope and lightness, when the guilt was too embedded or the trauma too deep, was common. And I knew it. But I needed this as much as he did.

"Do you think your wife would feel like you'd forgotten her, Doug? Or do you think your wife would want you to move on?"

I knew the answer, because I'd read his files. His wife Maggie had passed after a long and painful battle with cancer. On her deathbed, she'd made him promise to stay with therapy, to do everything he could to live a happy life. She'd told him to find joy and to have the next adventure.

But Doug wasn't ready to face that. And I'd pushed too hard.

With one last scowl, he rose and left the room without another word. The dark, sad, but familiar pressure of failure clamped over my heart.

"I'll see you next week, Doug."

I wasn't sure why I told the empty room that, but it churned inside me like it was true. Was that the power of being a word witch? Could I use it to compel people to open up, to return and seek the treatment they needed? I didn't want to manipulate their emotions, but I needed to understand my power on a deeper level.

Later. This session had been a failure, but it was just the first one. I had an entire day full of patients to work through.

What could go wrong?

CHAPTER FOURTEEN

Everything went wrong.

From the dragon shifter whose wife was threatening to leave him unless he got his hoarding tendencies under control to the troll with imposter syndrome, I maneuvered through my sessions trying to gracefully accept the supernatural I hadn't known existed weirdly melded with modern problems.

I encouraged patients to use the chair, and most of them did. That should have been a good sign that there was a willingness to progress. But all they wanted to do was talk. And they didn't want to talk to me.

Any attempt at alternative tools, or for them to see past their issues, ended in frustration and doubt.

The dragon even set the couch on fire.

I stumbled through each session, trying to use my alleged word power to make breakthroughs and reach to the core of their issues. If I could get one of my new clients to see their time with me as a positive, I figured that would be a start.

I had to admit, though, that the challenge was nice. It was the first time in a hot minute that I'd actually enjoyed my work.

Even though, as I closed the door on my first day, I felt like a complete failure.

"Why the sour puss?" Brianne slung her purse over her shoulder and turned off the light over the reception desk. "Rough day?"

"I never in a million years would have planned a day like this." I followed her out the front door. "I can't seem to connect to any of my patients."

"Well, I'm not one to counsel the counselor but Agatha always said the most crucial component to a good therapy practice was trust." Brianne gave my forearm a reassuring squeeze. "That takes time."

"I suppose." I leaned against the porch as she descended the stairs. This close, the dilapidated facade of the house still held, and I couldn't quite believe it was the same beautiful estate I'd just walked out of. Why did the house maintain such a pristine interior but look so shoddy on the outside?

"It's not just that my methodologies are different from Agatha's. There's a wall between me and my patients. It's the supernatural thing."

"You're a witch, Simone." She turned to face me from the bottom of the stairs. "You're supernatural, too. You're just not used to it yet."

"I don't know that I'll ever be." There was a whiny petulance in my tone I couldn't quite lose. "It's not normal." Her body tensed, and with a fidget she checked her watch. "Sorry, you're on a timetable. Gotta pick the kids up?"

"My youngest ones are about to get out of school." She beamed like a proud momma. "I like to walk home with them on Mondays. It's a nice way to start the week."

"I totally understand." My heart jolted in my chest. "I used to pick up my son on Fridays for bubble tea."

Well, at least the petulance was gone from my tone. Outright sorrow took its place. I tried to swallow down the surge of pain. To breathe through the rush of guilt that settled in my stomach, poisoning me as if I'd bitten into a thermometer and swallowed the mercury within.

"Simone?" Brianne rushed to me. "What's wrong?"

"Nothing. No, I'm fine. I just ... it's been a long day." I was trembling and sweaty, like a virus engulfed me. But Brianne had kids to get to, and I didn't want to talk about Gabe. I'd had enough failure for one day.

"House, could I trouble you for a glass of water?" It arrived in my hand, cool and crisp. Brianne lifted an eyebrow in shock, but didn't say anything further. I drank it down, motioning her away. "Go pick up your kiddos. I'll see you tomorrow."

"I'm looking forward to our dinner Friday night, Simone." Brianne gave me what I now considered her patented compassionate smile. "I think it might do you some good to see what a *normal* family looks like in Treater's Way."

Female friendships were a difficult thing to maneuver once you reached a certain age. I'd had college friends, my old roommate and a girl who'd been my lab partner senior year, but they were surface-level relationships at best. Jeff and I had couple-friends as well, but I never saw the partners outside of group outings.

Having someone to talk to would be really, really nice. And she was right, like always. It would do me good to enjoy something mundane, even if I hated that word.

"I'd really like that."

As she hurried off, I scraped at a bit of chipped wood on the banister. The house looked so different on the outside. I didn't understand if that was by choice, or if that had to do with its dwindling magic supplies while it held two Ephemeral Supremes in place.

"House, do you supply my magic, or do I give you some of my own?" I don't know why I expected an answer. I sat at the aged rocker, taking a sip from the water glass that was now full again. "I love the lack of humidity you've created. I guess, when I think about it, we all feel different on the inside, don't we? Some folks are better at masking it, but ultimately, it's still a mask.

I let my eyes drift closed, enjoying the calm of a small town. No cars sped past. No horns honked. Occasionally, a gaggle of mothers with their children passed by. They'd wave and smile, then continue on their way.

It was peaceful. Not that I could hold onto that peace. Grabbing my phone, I scrolled to my text messages with Gabe. He wasn't answering them. I couldn't blame him.

I'd been so distraught when I caught Jeff cheating. And alone. Without a friend to rely on, I'd called the last person I should have reached out to. That conversation did not go well.

"I really want to repair what I broke with you, son." I murmured the words aloud as I typed and sent them, tears dripping onto my screen. With a hasty wipe, I set it aside, hoping to latch onto the peace in the air surrounding me.

"THIMONE! WHERE THE THUCK ARE YOU?"

I bolted out of my chair at the rusty creak of the front gate opening.

Jeff stumbled into the yard, barely taking two steps before he yelped in pain. Locking eyes wilder than his hair with me, he jabbed a swollen hand in my direction.

"YOU CRAZY BITH!"

Jeff looked like he hadn't slept in a week, which I had to admit gave me a little bit of glee. He wasn't wearing shoes. Crusted mud and something I couldn't identify caked his toes. His feet were red and puffy, as if he walked around barefoot all the time.

He bared his teeth when our eyes met. In the gape of his mouth, his tongue shone silver. Droplets of dried blood coated his chin.

"UNDO THITH THIMONE! WHAT DID YOU DO TO ME? THOODOO?"

Thoodoo? I didn't even know what that was.

Force of habit had me rushing down the steps to tend to him. But there was something in his expression, an untamed rage I'd never seen before, that held me back. I stopped at the base and held out one hand.

"Jeff, what's happened to you?" He marched forward, tripping and landing on his knees with a loud *oof.* "I didn't do this. How could I?"

There was an odd sense of doubt in my voice. I hadn't done this, had I? The memory of Gumbo and me at my mother's grave flitted back. *Be careful, Simone. Your words have power.*

Was thoodoo ... voodoo? Jeff thought I'd cursed him. I took in his disheveled appearance and filthy clothes. I'd wished his clothes would stay dirty forever. I'd wished he'd bite his silver tongue every time he spoke.

He was on his feet again, struggling to reach me. A foul stench, sour bile days old, wafted toward me with each step. Oh, no. I'd hoped he would step in vomit every time he tried to wear shoes.

I *had* cursed him. A bubble of laughter popped on my lips, the sound so hysterical I was surprised it was mine. I clamped my hand over my mouth, hoping he hadn't heard. His glare told me he had.

"YOU WILL PAY FOR THIS, THIMONE!"

Jeff attempted to lunge at me, his hands outstretched like claws. I didn't have time to feel bad for what I'd done. My pulse leapt into my throat, and instinct took over. I turned and bolted up the stairs, running for the front door.

"House, do not let him in!"

My hand froze on the doorknob when I heard the growl. It was the most terrifying sound I'd ever encountered. My hair stood on end. A chill covered my body. I turned in slow motion.

The wolf from the graveyard stood at the stairs between Jeff and me. It flicked one glance in my direction, meeting my eyes. Once again, I had the sense I was looking at eyes I'd seen before. A shocking pool of lust landed in my belly. Its salt and pepper fur bristled, as if it felt it too.

"H-hi." Let it never be said that I'm cool under pressure.

The wolf dipped its head, almost like a greeting, then turned away from me. Planting all fours, it faced Jeff squarely and growled again. When I say I felt that growl down to my roots, it's not an exaggeration. It was most definitely the kind of warning meant to strike fear.

And it worked. I was terrified.

So was Jeff. He went completely still. The front of his filthy slacks darkened with urine. I couldn't blame him. I wanted to pee my pants, too. He backed up, which seemed like a terrible idea. With a stumble, he landed on his ass. The wolf descended the stairs with deliberate slowness. Jeff was being stalked.

There was a lot going on. I couldn't pull many clear thoughts from my brain. I opened my mouth to speak, and a weird kind of squeak came out. I pinched the space between my thumb and forefinger, willing my brain to focus. Somehow, I knew I was safe with the wolf.

But Jeff wasn't. No matter how angry I was, I couldn't allow him to be hurt.

"Jeff, you should leave. And you are not invited back here."

Jeff's near-delirious eyes lifted to mine. His lip raised in a snarl. Was he actually snarling at me with a giant wolf ready to eat him?

"This will all be gone in the morning." I waved my hand to encompass the mess that was my husband. "Just go."

He backed his way to the gate, using it as leverage to stand.

"This ithn't over, Thimone."

Once he was on the other side, he ran, his yelps of pain fading with the distance.

"No, this isn't over, Jeff. But we are." My throat was almost too tight to swallow. Fresh tears drenched my cheeks.

The wolf turned to face me, whimpering in my direction. The bristles of his fur softened. I don't know why, but my fingers itched to stroke him. Everything inside me was black and unsettled. Burying myself in this creature felt like the safest place in the world. The wolf's eyes turned down, as if my sadness had become his.

"Thank you for not hurting him," I said. "And, uh, for protecting me." He held my eyes a moment longer. In a single leap, he was over the gate and headed in the direction Jeff had run. Without asking, I knew he'd make sure Jeff left town.

I didn't want to walk through the house in case someone was in the lobby, not that I'd ever seen anyone entering or leaving. Instead, I followed the side path to the curved stairs. Gumbo sat at the top, a charcoal gray bow on his neck.

I reached down to scratch under his chin, only then realizing how badly I was shaking.

"We have excellent security at the Magnolia," Gumbo said, threading his way around my legs.

Once I was inside the house, my knees gave out. I sank to the floor, head against the door for support, as if it might hold me up while I figured things out.

Which might have been true. After what I'd just seen, there was no way I could question magic.

Or my abilities.

After all, I'd managed to hex my ex without even realizing it.

What other damage had I done?

CHAPTER FIFTEEN

A good therapist knows how to compartmentalize. Even when they are suffering under the weight of personal struggles, they stuff their own needs into a tiny box in their hearts, lock stray thoughts in a cabinet in their brains, and focus on their patients.

Sure, they might mention feeling out of sorts, but only in a way that conveys humanity. They are meant to have feelings, but not express them. It's important that therapists have personal boundaries. That they keep their biases in check and provide a safe and judgment-free space for whoever sat on their proverbial couch.

Funny how, only yesterday morning, I'd believed I'd ever been a good therapist.

One day later, sitting across from a fire nymph with post-traumatic stress, I had doubts about, well, pretty much everything. When she'd introduced herself, I'd been unable to hide the sheer exhaustion that had clawed so deep into me no amount of rest would release it.

I'd gone to bed resolved to embrace the magic in the world around me. But by morning, my resolve had faded. I was more out of sorts than ever, and the events of the day before still held me in place.

When my first client sauntered in, with glowing skin and hair that resembled being engulfed in flames, the shock hit me afresh. Aside from the Twins, who I hadn't seen since the board meeting, every other supernatural encounter had an aura of normality to it. Sure, someone can *say* they were a troll or dragon. But when they look human, it's easier to believe that's part of the delusion.

I could rationalize Gumbo talking to me as part of my imagination. And the wolf from last night? That ...

Nope. That one stayed in its mental box for now.

But there was no way I could pretend the female sitting across from me, who claimed to be a fire nymph by the name of Cindrette, was human. Despite my efforts to compartmentalize, flashes of the night before invaded my every thought.

The silver of her skin reflected the strange color I'd turned Jeff's tongue.

She spoke in short bursts, afraid to let her words come out. Not unlike me.

And she wore no shoes, though her feet were blessedly free of vomit. In fact, they were clean and manicured, tucked underneath her legs. She'd chosen the chair, and that small win was enough to dissolve me into tears. I recovered. Eventually. And apologized. Profusely.

But it wasn't the best first impression. And here I was, thirty minutes later, still dwelling on it rather than listening to her talk.

Oh, yeah. I'm nailing this therapy thing.

"I jolt awake in the middle of the night, terrified I'm still under her thrall. I've even awoken a few times half altered." She dropped her voice, eyes darting from side to side as if someone might hear her and pounce. "I set one of the rooms in Bridge House on fire. In my sleep!"

"That must have been very stressful for you. How was that resolved?"

"Oh, you know Bridge House." Cindrette shook her head. An actual tinder flitted from her hair, crackling as it popped out of existence. "Misty took care of it. It's not the room that scared me. It's that I hadn't been aware I'd changed."

I made a note in my notepad. I *didn't* know about Bridge House. Or Misty. But my tour of the town had referenced the tiny island connected to Illusion Square by a bridge and the B&B run by a mermaid.

And it had the same air of familiarity to it I was growing used to. An annoying, but near-constant, sense of deja vu. I've seen this before. I've been across the bridge and onto the island. And something happened there.

Something I needed to pry out of its mental box. I pinched the space between my thumb and forefinger again, reminding myself I was trying to be a good therapist.

"Let's talk about the moments you feel safe, Cindrette. Can you recall any of them for me right now?"

"Safe?" Her dark orange brows furrowed low over eyes that glowed like embers.

"Yeah, you know, the moments you aren't looking over your shoulder."

She tilted her head, as if examining the strange woman asking questions in the hopes of understanding her. Good luck with that one, Cindy old gal, I barely understand myself.

"Is there something about my suggestion that is making you feel unsafe, Cindrette?"

"What? Oh, no!" Bless it, I could feel the wave of anxiety cascading through her. The people pleaser in me understood it completely. "It's not that at all. I just thought ..."

She waggled her fingers in the air. Try as I might, it was not a gesture I could interpret.

"I'm sorry, Cindrette. Can you communicate your concern to me?" I faked a smile. "I promise I won't be upset, no matter what you say."

Yuck. My stomach churned. I'd said something I didn't mean, and my body didn't like it. I kept the smile plastered on while Cindrette fidgeted in her chair. Finally, she cast her glance out the window.

"Don't you want to hear about The Battle? Agatha always wanted me to talk about The Battle."

I bit back an exhausted sigh. Several years ago, there'd been some sort of fight for Illusion Square. Several of my patients referenced it, giving their versions of how they'd participated. I understood the need for them to share the tragedy.

All of us who grew up in the area had a hurricane story. We used them when we met to gauge one another. Who's your momma and can you make a roux, as the natives would say. Where were you for the big storm?

The Battle was Treater's Way's version of Katrina. *I was in the Square when the fire started. I'd just left Explore Art before the shooting started. I worked with so-and-so and they ...*

It went on and on. The Battle mattered to the town, and I had to respect that. And those who'd fought in it had trauma galore. I was here to help them.

For a town with so much potential, too many of its residents dwelled on the past.

"Do you feel like you want to talk about The Battle again?"

She gnawed on her ruby red lips, entwining her fingers like she was tying a knot. Countless sessions with Agatha, she'd done just that. Relived the horror of being trapped in a dragon form. Forced to use her power to destroy the very things she loved and revered. Her own will shut down as someone else manipulated her for their benefit.

What she'd gone through was clearly traumatic. She was struggling to move forward, even years later. She couldn't sleep or relax. She didn't have a permanent place to call home.

And every week, that fact was reiterated without the benefit of hope or action. She reminded herself of her trauma. Lived in it, day after day.

It was another example of Agatha's talk methods being ineffective.

Cindrette's lips trembled. The muscles in her long, silver neck tensed. I wasn't sure if she knew she was holding live fire in her hand, but I didn't want to ask. Its heat waved the space between us. I braced myself, in case she spontaneously combusted or turned into a dragon.

As quickly as it had flamed, the fire was gone. She squared herself to face me, planting her feet on the ground.

"No. No, I do not want to talk about the past anymore. I want to figure out how to live in the now. I want a future!" Her tiny voice faltered, but her eyes held firm.

A spark of hope lit within. A desperately needed sign of progress.

"Good." My next smile was neither fake nor forced. "So, let's start by finding the moments you feel safe and start from there."

Thirty minutes later, Cindrette clutched the new journal I'd given her tight to her chest and rose to leave. "This was so helpful, thank you! I can't wait to get started. Right after my next appointment."

"Next appointment?" I walked her out, scanning the lobby for Brianne but finding it empty.

"With Lydia." A deep purple blush rose in Cindrette's cheeks. "I have a standing treatment right next door."

She scurried to the Med Spa door and swung it open. I caught a glimpse of pristine white walls and light chatter before the door closed again. My phone pinged. A message from Brianne that she'd left to run an errand and that my next two patients had already canceled.

Word was already spreading. And not the way I wanted it to.

Perhaps it was time I made my presence known in the other divisions. Time to get a feel for the business side of this crazy inheritance.

I had two hours with no work and the contact high of a productive session. Eyeing the Med Spa sign, I stalked to the door and yanked on the handle. Maybe the positive energy of Cindrette greeting me would help fuel the kind of gossip I *did* want. If nothing else, Lydia would see that I knew how to do my damn job.

Even if I wasn't totally convinced.

CHAPTER
SIXTEEN

I walked into a smaller waiting area. It was clean and cozy. The white I thought I'd seen on the walls turned out to be a soft taupe. There was a row of seating—lavender chairs that matched Lydia's hair and looked ridiculously comfy. Glass shelves with gold accents housed an assortment of bottles with the same label I recognized from my living space.

Despite Cindrette walking in only a minute before me, the space was empty. Except for Lydia. She hovered over a small standing desk in the center of the room, in front of a wide curtain that spanned wall to wall. When she lifted her creamsicle eyes to greet me, a bolt of lightning shot through my body.

The small buzz of hope and excitement I'd felt at my first successful session amplified. I went from giddy to outright drunk with pride in seconds. This was different from the sensation I'd experienced in the boardroom. That had been a stream of blissful acceptance.

This was an ocean of champagne at high tide. A hiccup escaped my lips. I covered them with a shocked giggle. Lydia's calm face lifted into a mischievous grin.

"Good morning, Simone. I was wondering when you'd find your way to us. Can I offer you a drink?" She gestured toward the compact water jug in the far corner. Slices of cucumber and leafy green mint floated in the crystal-clear water.

Suddenly, I was parched. It took all I had not to cross the room and lift the jug directly to my mouth. Instead, with shaky legs, I did what I hoped was a cool stride over to it.

"I can get my own water, thank you." My words were slurring, and my head held the fog of a hangover. Weird. I thought I would feel *good* in the medspa. Instead, I just felt ... topsy-turvy.

"As you wish, Ephemeral Supreme." Lydia's grin stretched from ear to ear.

A small voice inside me shrieked in protest, and the house groaned. It was at least a hundred years old, as far as I knew, and I'd never heard that sound before. The floorboards never creaked when you walked across them. The house didn't "settle" the way others did. The sound of it happening was jarring enough to snap me back into reality.

And once there, I was right pissed off at Lydia Langley.

Part of my training as a therapist had been learning to embrace that emotions, by themselves, are neutral. Feeling pain isn't automatically a bad thing. Joy is great, but sadness has its place in our lives as well. Logically, I knew that.

But in this case, I latched on to the growing rage pooling in my stomach and let it take charge of my voice.

"This bullshit manipulation of my emotions stops now, Lydia. Not only is it rude and disrespectful, but it's violating as well. We won't have that at the Magnolia. Am I clear?"

Whoa. Once the words were out, everything underneath my feet shifted. If I'd been floating before, I was surely on solid ground now.

Lydia's face barely registered her shock, but it rode off her in waves. The smile disappeared. One lovely eyebrow lifted. And a surge of anger that matched my own knocked me back a step. It came at me like an animal poised to attack its prey. I widened my stance to brace myself.

Lauren had implied the Twins were fae. I didn't know much about them other than what I'd read in a few of my favorite fantasy novels. But I remembered reading that they were strong. Super strong. And fast. Lydia could have crossed the room in a heartbeat and broken my neck.

But even as the thought latched onto me, the force of her anger barreling forward stopped short inches from my body. It curled there like invisible smoke. Tentatively, I extended one hand and met a wall.

So I had a barrier. Interesting.

Lydia's lip lifted into a snarl, and the anger slinked back to its owner.

"I don't want to fight with you Lydia." I inched sideways and sank into one of the chairs. My butt sighed in bliss as it conformed to my body. With a gesture, I motioned to the chair beside me. "Why don't we try talking instead?"

"Five minutes." She tapped her delicate wrist, which incidentally did not have a watch, and crossed the room to join me with a weightless grace I envied. I tended to clomp about, my steps heavy.

Up close, she was even more beautiful. Her skin was flawless. She tucked her hair behind one ear with long, slender fingers. A cascade of gold cuffed the ear, which tapered to a sharp point at the top. Her skin was milk dipped in honey. When she moved, the crisp scent of bergamot followed.

"Are you and Lyra the creators of the beauty line I have upstairs?" She tilted her head at me, as if she didn't understand the question. "You smell like bergamot. It reminds me of the product upstairs with that logo over there."

She inspected me for a moment, pursing her lips together. When she answered, her voice was no longer the lilting melody from before. Instead, it was clipped and guarded.

"It was Lyra's idea. We took it to Agatha, and she let us run a trial." A hint of her smile returned. "It was a very successful trial."

"I saw the YouTube page. Two million followers. I even used it to put on makeup." When she only stared at me as if I was being analyzed, I continued. "I like it. That's all I'm saying. I'm not trying to be your enemy."

She thawed. It was the slightest drop of her shoulders, but the air between us softened. Not a lot. I could work with that.

"If you want us to get along, stop using your magic against others." She leaned back, looking at me over her long nose. "And schedule a facial. Your skin is atrocious."

I was too shocked by the former to be offended by the latter.

"I'm not using my magic against anyone," I told her. But dammit. There it was in my voice again. A hint of a tremor that told me I was lying. Even to myself.

"Is that so?" Lydia, of course, picked up on it. "I suppose your husband just woke up with a strange virus that coincided with your cruel oaths to him? And you walked in here telling me what is allowed at the Magnolia because you have such a strong sense of authority and not because you know I have to obey?"

Had I thought she'd softened toward me? Hah. The anger prowled around me once more. Lydia rose to her feet and paced the small space of the waiting room.

"And the trick you played on poor Doug Holloway yesterday?" She uttered a scoff. "Really, Simone, I didn't expect you to stoop so low. Especially on your first day."

"I what? What did I do?" My mind was a jumbled mess, trying to reconcile what she was saying about my session with Doug. "I didn't play any tricks, Lydia. I was using a therapy tool that is useful when ..."

My words trailed off at her self-righteous glare. She planted her hands on her hips. It was the most expressive I'd ever seen her.

"You aren't fooling me, Simone. And you certainly didn't fool Doug." Then she laughed, and it was nothing short of a witch's cackle. "Once word got around that you tried to manipulate his emotions, to use your expression, you were sunk."

She peeked behind the curtain, offering me a glimpse of what appeared to be an endless hallway with rows of doors on each side. A light above a door at least a mile away flickered green.

"My client is ready. Unlike you, I take care of their needs rather than my own."

I had no response. I was too dumbfounded to defend myself. She slid behind the curtain without saying goodbye. But her follow-up words bounced through the room and filled my head.

"Stop trying so hard to make an impact. You're only losing our respect more." Her laughter echoed in my ears. "Then again, maybe don't stop. In thirty days, you'll be out of here, and we can all move on. Whether we want to or not."

I sat in the waiting room with my mouth gaping open. Whether they want to or not? What did that even mean?

It had only been a few days. But I was screwing this up. Majorly. And for the first time, I realized that the consequences of my failure didn't just affect me and Agatha. The other division heads had something at stake.

Frustration cut through my haze. If they had something to lose, why not help me? Why mess with me and test me instead of showing me compassion and guiding me? Aside from Brianne, no one was reaching out. I had no details and no idea where to get them.

Maybe they were just busy. Maybe, despite never seeing anyone come in or go out, business was better than I realized. I'd never asked Ethan for financials, nor had he offered them. Then again, I hadn't asked.

I'd made the decision to focus on the therapy division. The job I was supposed to know how to do.

Part of me wanted to stomp behind that curtain and bang on every door until I found Lydia. Then I'd give her a piece of my mind, consequences be damned. I'd just sat there while she accused me of things I hadn't even done. I deserved to defend myself.

But disturbing every client at the spa didn't make good business sense. And, as much as I was loath to admit it, Lydia was right. At least partly. I had hexed Jeff, even if it was unintentional. Gumbo warned me to be careful about my words. I'd done the opposite.

But Doug? All I wanted was to help him. I'd definitely never played a trick on him, intentional or otherwise.

Had I?

I rose with a sigh, taking my glass of water and leaving it right next to Lydia's computer just for spite. I stuck my tongue out at the curtain and returned to my office.

And sat. All afternoon. While session after session either called and canceled or didn't bother to show.

By the end of day two, I'd seen exactly one patient, gotten into a fight with a colleague, and learned the town was already turning against me based on something I didn't even know I'd done.

And I had no idea what to do about any of it.

Panic crept into my veins, turning my blood to ice. My heartbeat quickened until my pulse pounded along my neck. I tried to take calming breaths, but with each inhale, my situation clamped harder onto my chest. I dug tingling fingers into my palms and squeezed my eyes shut.

The urge to vomit surged through me. I'd never make it to a restroom. I yanked the rusted copper trash can at my feet and hauled it on my lap, leaning over it as my body shuddered and heaved.

Another panic attack. There was no way I would be able to talk myself out of this one. I needed help.

"Gumbo."

The heavy vibration of Gumbo's purrs rumbled all the way up to my stomach. He rubbed against me, pushing his head into my fisted hands until they relaxed. He whispered to me, and I clung to his fur until my heartbeat slowed and my breath was deep.

When I opened my eyes, I was no longer in my office. And I wasn't alone.

CHAPTER SEVENTEEN

"It's okay." Brianne made a shushing sound in a soothing tone while she rubbed my back. "You aren't alone, Simone. It's going to be okay."

"Is it?" I was still heaving, my body shaking with sobs. The trash pail was gone, and we were sitting on the red couch in my living room. Or what was currently my living room. It wouldn't be in thirty days. Because I was a complete failure and was going to screw up and end up homeless, divorced, and—

"Stop." Brianne's tone no longer consoled me. It was sharp and harsh and stopped my runaway thoughts in their tracks. "I don't know what you're thinking but stop it right now."

"And whatever it is, don't say it out loud." Gumbo weaved his way through my feet. "No more careless use of words, Simone."

On a rational level, I knew they were right. But my emotions still held control. It took time. Water. Breath. Support.

Eventually, the world came back into focus around me.

"How'd I get here?" Across from us, the wooden rocker creaked as it swayed. A crocheted blanket in bold blue was draped across the seat, as if covering someone's lap. But the chair appeared empty.

"House brought you to me." Gumbo hopped between Brianne and me and settled on the couch. "We didn't want to risk anyone seeing you in the lobby."

"I've never seen anyone in the lobby." I flounced backward to sink into the cushions and whine. "I haven't seen a single customer since I got here."

"That doesn't mean they aren't there, Sweets," Brianne said.

My breath caught in my throat. Sweets had been the term of affection my mother used for me. Hearing Brianne use it created a swirl of new emotions. I missed having guidance and a strong, steady presence in my life. I missed someone being casually affectionate with me because I mattered to them.

I dug my head deeper into the plush cushion behind me, self-pity shrouding me in a dark cloud so thick I could almost see it.

"What happens if I fail at the end of thirty days, Gumbo? Do you know?"

"I do." Gumbo hopped on my lap, placing a paw on each shoulder and holding my eyes. I could not think of anything more disconcerting. "The magic held by Agatha and the house will be returned to the Mighty Oak. It will disperse it as it feels necessary."

"There's more," Brianne chimed in. "The Twins are technically on loan to our realm. Sort of like a work visa. They will be forced to return."

"That's right." Gumbo hopped off my lap and snuggled closer to Brianne. "And all of the good we can do at the Magnolia will be whisked away."

Whoa. So, no pressure there. If I leaned in to the repercussions, a small thread of panic rose in my chest. What would happen to Lauren? To the patients I had not seen because they didn't trust me yet? No wonder the Twins were so hostile. I held their future in my hands.

"Great." I sunk deeper into the couch, like it might swallow me whole, crossing my arms with a hefty pout.

"But you won't let that happen, Sweets." Brianne gave me her signature supportive smile. "You've got everything you need inside you. You just have to embrace it."

Embrace it. I couldn't remember being embraced in ages. Or having someone believe in me and call me Sweets. I closed my eyes, trying to fight off the sense of despair

When was the last time Jeff said anything remotely kind to me? Or looked at me like anything other than a roommate? And though I'd been the one to stab the heart of my relationship with my son, we'd been distant for years before he severed ties.

I couldn't pinpoint when I'd checked out of my own life. Maybe it wasn't an exact moment. Maybe, over time, I'd taken on the roles expected of me and performed them adequately. Wife. Mother. Therapist.

But had I ever truly embraced any of them? Nope.

I'd been on autopilot. Going through the motions.

The only time I truly *felt* anything was when a panic attack engulfed me. And that was not the life I wanted for myself. Not anymore.

Something stirred, deep in my core. I had it inside me. I'd seen hints of it, hadn't I?

I sat up, waving my hand around, as if the cloud were truly surrounding me. As if I were clearing a fog. As if I were blowing away the stank in the room.

Brianne still sat nearby while I disappeared inside my thoughts, prepared to comfort. Gumbo, the mystical protector, his silky-smooth fur warm against my thigh, had jumped to my aid more than once.

Maybe the Twins weren't on my side, but they still needed me to succeed. And the two here now believed in me. I felt certain Lauren and Ethan would support me. Plus, I had a giant wolf on my side. Maybe.

I wasn't alone anymore.

I'd made mistakes. A ton of them. I couldn't say whether I could correct them all.

But I sure as shit wanted to try. After all, I had nothing left to lose.

The blanket on the rocker shifted before drifting to the floor. Why did it look familiar? Where had I seen that before? It wasn't the blanket itself that drew me in, it was the color ...

Then, it hit me.

"I'll be right back." I darted off the couch and down the hallway to the bedroom.

It had been the first room to truly call to me. The first to comfort me. This time, when I entered and really paid attention to the design, I finally understood why. The bedroom I was living in today was an updated, adult version of the bedroom I'd had as a child.

At the foot of the bed was a new piece of furniture, one that wasn't there when I first got here. It was a blanket chest with chipped corners and a scratched surface.

Okay, so, it wasn't new. Not exactly. It carried layers of paint from the times I'd redecorated. It had once been the same soft greens as this room. In college, I'd painted it pastel pink and used a store-bought stencil to add brightly colored tulips.

When Jeff and I bought a house, I'd painted it blue. The same color as the items I'd shoved inside.

I dropped to my knees in front of it, lifting the top—remembering at the last second it tended to swing closed on my fingers—and reaching inside to drag out the contents.

A few of my mother's favorite books. A picture album. A necklace I carried around but never wore or got rid of.

And the Blue Hoard.

Musty piles of scarves. A dozen tea cozies. Pot holders. There used to be a blanket, but it was apparently in the living room now.

I'd mentioned them to Doug during our session, using them as a tool to create a connection with him. Looking at them now, I let the grief of the memories they carried wash over me.

I wished I'd mentioned that part to him. I wished I'd let him see they weren't a tool. Rather than using it as a connection to the present, I should have let him see my grief over the past.

That, even after thirty years, it fades away yet remains. Like a scar. The sharp sting of the gash was far more painful, but the memory of it can bring the pain to light. Each time you see the scar, you remember the pain anew. Distantly. It doesn't have the ability to open wounds.

It stays with you, as it should. And, once healed, it becomes part of you. A new skin you carry forever while you march forward.

To create new scars.

I'd held myself back from sharing that with Doug. Over the years, I'd wanted to offer up personal anecdotes to my patients. I'd wanted to go beyond the tools and create true connection. Traditional therapy felt hollow to me. Even modern methods created a distance I didn't understand.

They didn't need my problems. I didn't need to blur boundaries. But they needed to know I understood them. Really understood them. Because I had been through my own wars.

Instead, I'd stifled my voice to do what I thought was expected. I'd tried too hard to *look* like I was creating a connection that I'd actually severed any hopes of one.

I'd become ineffective because I'd ignored my voice.

My voice. Which was apparently where my power came from.

Wouldn't using it help me transform into the therapist I truly longed to be? Maybe trusting what my soul longed to say out loud was the key to turning things around.

If only I knew how.

I rushed back to the living room where Brianne scratched behind Gumbo's ear.

"Gumbo, can you show me how to use my power?"

Gumbo opened one eye. A hint of a smile lifted his cute little mug. He stretched his paws and went back to sleep.

"My power is my voice, right? I need to understand it better."

Gumbo sighed and stood, turned in a circle, then curled closer to Brianne, who watched our exchange in amused silence.

Exasperation swelled in my chest, clogging my throat until I could not swallow. Had I just thought Gumbo would be helpful? Why was he ignoring me?

"Gumbo? Will you please help me?"

Gumbo's tail twitched, but it was the only sign he'd heard me. As adorable as he was, I wanted to yank his sparkly gold bow right off his neck and stomp on it. I looked to Brianne, lifting my hands to the sky in a WTF gesture.

"Maybe he wants you to use your words more carefully, Simone." She held the hint of a smile as well, making me even angrier.

I was about to tell them to forget it, that I would do it myself. Then the rocker creaked again. As I turned to it, the blanket still on the floor lifted and draped over an invisible lap.

"Oh, good." I chewed on the inside of my cheek. "Agatha is watching me, too."

A breeze sharper than ice crystals slapped me in the face. It didn't hurt—I don't think it was intended to—but it was certainly a wakeup call. I heard a distinctive voice in my head scream *use your words*.

Oh.

I needed to be careful with my words. That made sense. What can I say? Sometimes, I'm a little slow. Especially when emotions are involved.

I closed my eyes, channeling all my breath into my throat to soothe and release the pressure. I waited for the right words to float to the top. Then, I simply released them into the air.

"Gumbo, Mystical Protector of Magnolia, you will help the

Ephemeral Supreme Simone, not Agatha, to understand her powers and use them with purpose."

Brianne clapped so hard I took an amused bow. What a joy it was to have a friend in my corner.

"Okay." Gumbo stood, arching his back into a deep stretch. "What would you like to learn first?"

I took a moment to think about his question. I had hexes to undo and mistakes to rectify. But I wanted to be sure I did those right. I wanted something basic. A small win that would boost my confidence and help me understand myself better.

When the answer came, my entire body tingled with it.

"I know just where to start."

CHAPTER EIGHTEEN

Outside the Magnolia, someone had mowed the small patches of grass on either side of our walkway. Either that or the house was able to keep it trimmed. From the board meeting, I had a vague recollection of Lydia or Lyra mentioning that House did the gardening. Maybe House was all-purpose.

Or maybe that nice, terrifying wolf with the hauntingly familiar eyes had done it.

Surveying the house much as I had on my first day, I found it hard to fight the urge to fix the entire thing. It needed a massive overhaul. But I didn't trust myself to do that much.

"Brianne, you said I couldn't see everyone in the lobby earlier, right?"

"That's right." She gnawed on her lower lip, her brow furrowing. "I think, maybe, you're not trusted enough to see everything as it is yet."

Ouch. I can see why she was nervous to say that. I rubbed at my heart.

"That's fair, I suppose. I've only been here for like five days, and so far ... I'm not off to a great start, am I?"

"You'll fix it." She linked our arms.

I wasn't sure why she had so much faith in me, but I would take it. I needed all the faith I could get. In my head, I grabbed for one of my favorite songs, singing it to myself.

They said, "Babe, you gotta fake it 'til you make it" and I did.

Okay, Simone. It was time to fake it.

"So, what do you see in front of us?"

"The same thing you see, Simone." Gumbo weaved through my legs with a soothing purr. "House is focusing all its magic inside right now. It's barely covering the gardens."

Hmm. So someone else was mowing the front lawn. I'd investigate that mystery another time.

For now, I wanted to focus my energies on the house, on something I could give it that would satisfy both of our needs at the moment.

"Last week when I first got here, I looked at the house with all this fear and the feeling of being overwhelmed and said something strange out loud."

"What was it?" Gumbo ceased his weaving and sat near my feet, looking up at me.

"Something about clouds gathering but the sun coming out. I don't remember it. I wasn't paying attention." I managed an awkward grin when Gumbo rolled his eyes. I had no idea a cat could roll its eyes.

"Anyway, I do remember saying that I would receive a sign that things would work out." I dipped my head to Brianne's shoulder. "Then you stepped outside and welcomed me."

"Aww." Brianne grabbed me into a fierce hug. How could I possibly let this woman down? The fear welled again, rolling in my stomach like I'd swallowed a million flies.

"Focus, Simone." Gumbo batted at my foot to get my attention. "The most important part of accessing your ability is to focus it."

"How did you know I wasn't focused?"

"Let's just say you should never play poker."

I snorted. Jeff had always admonished me in public, telling me to turn down my face. Maybe I wasn't as good at masking how I felt as I thought I was.

Gumbo pounced on a small ant traveling across the cobblestone, picking it up to inspect it between his tiny gold claws. With a flick of his tongue, the ant disappeared. He returned to me.

"Anyway, it's time to focus."

"What do I do?"

"Pay attention to your breath. Quiet your mind and really listen to what your instincts are telling you." He weaved between my legs again.

His *I Can Haz* voice softened. It became deeper. As he instructed me to breathe, his purrs reminded me of a rich baritone. There was a fullness to his tone that reminded me of other worlds and a cosmos filled with magic.

I closed my eyes, shutting out the dilapidated look of the house and picturing, instead, the house I saw in my memories. I tried to practice the deep, throat-constricting breath I'd learned in a yoga class one time. Instead of soothing me, it reminded me of inflexibility and competition.

I was never a good yogi. Or yogini. Whatever they called the woman.

"Simone, you must focus." It was as if Gumbo were behind me, in my ear rather than at my feet. His whiskers tickled my neck, and I gave it a scratch.

"Right, sorry." With a shake of my head, I freed my breathing. Yoga breath wasn't right for me. What about box breathing? It was a calming technique my patients loved. And a social media favorite. Might be worth a try.

I inhaled for a four-count. Held for a four-count. Exhaled for a four-count. Held again.

My heart beat a little faster, and the world around me tunneled. I gasped for air, as if I'd been held underwater for minutes.

Okay. So. Not box breath.

"What if you tried just breathing like a normal person?" Brianne's helpful voice sounded oddly far away. I opened one eye to check she was still next to me. She was, and she smiled. "You're making yourself light-headed, Sweets. Just relax."

Just relax. Sure. I could do that.

But the more I tried to relax, the more tense I became. Trying not to think about breathing, it turned out, made it impossible to think about anything besides breathing. This was stupid. I was making it more difficult than it needed to be.

Gumbo continued his weaving, his voice somehow inside me and all around me at once. Brianne stroked my back and murmured encouragement. I stood there, my eyes squeezed shut, trying to find something.

Why was this so hard? I'd literally redecorated the waiting room with just a few thoughts and a little imagination. I hadn't done any special breathing or needed a cat and a bestie to lift me up. I'd known what I wanted, and I made it happen.

Why was that so hard?

The frustration of it was eating me inside. Louder than either of my friends was my inner critic, and she was a bitch. She whispered I was failing. She reminded me I'd been failing for years. She listed all my faults. She told me not to bother.

She was pissing me off.

"This is stupid. I don't need to focus on my breath. I just want us to have a professional damn sign hanging out here."

At Brianne's sharp gasp, I opened my eyes.

The house was still a mess. Faded paint and rotted shutters remained. But I'd done something.

The overhead porch railing had gotten an incidental refresh. Rust no longer covered the ornate railing. The old, warped sign with words crossed out was gone. In its place was a beautiful new sign. The edges rippled like waves.

A magnolia looked like it bloomed from the wood, its stem curling around one side, giving the entire sign a three-dimensional look that I absolutely adored.

Magnolia Therapy and Wellness Center adorned the middle, in ivory colored wording similar to the logo I'd seen on YouTube.

It was beautiful. It was perfect.

"It's just the beginning."

As if by magic, and maybe it was, my body settled. The anxiety within me stilled. I knew it was temporary, but the peace of it was something I could grab onto. A small win, just what I'd needed. But it turned out to be an even bigger win than I imagined.

"Whoa, nice sign!" Lauren exited the Magnolia and walked backwards along the path toward us to take it in. "That's gorgeous, Simone. Did you make that happen?"

"I did." I tried not to sound too proud of myself. In truth, I was exhausted. Between the panic attack, the roller coaster of emotions, and the verbal battle with Lydia that felt like it had happened a hundred years ago, I was worn out. "It took all I had, but I did it."

"Oh, you have more." Gumbo's voice was back to cute wittle kitty mode. "Well done." He sauntered back to the house and around the corner before I could even say thanks.

"You did great!" Brianne squeezed me close. "I knew you could do it. Now I have to run." Then she, too, scurried down the sidewalk, leaving Lauren and me alone.

"That was weird." I admired the sign. "Why didn't they stay and watch me gloat?"

"You can always gloat tomorrow." Lauren chuckled beside me. "Actually, they knew I wanted some time alone with you."

And just like that, the anxiety was back. Crap. I'd already had a run-in with one division head. I wasn't prepared for another yet. Couldn't I take my meager win and my dehydrated-from-crying-self inside, and feel good for ten, maybe fifteen minutes before pressure took over again? Was that so much to ask?

Apparently so.

"Let's go have a drink, Simone, and a good chat." I was still nervous, but Lauren's smile was pretty benign. "On me," she added.

"You're not gonna turn me into a toad or anything are you?"

Lauren dropped her pretty head back and laughed, loud and hard. It should have put me at ease. It should have, but it didn't.

"Not tonight," she replied with a wink. "In all seriousness, I want us to have a chance to talk and get to know each other again."

My head was spinning as I tried to come up with excuses why I couldn't go. But, as usual, instead of being productive, my brain froze under pressure. Just because she was mean to me in high school didn't mean she was still unkind. Ethan had said otherwise, and she'd been nice enough in the board meeting.

Besides, we were sort of partners now, and maybe a good time away from the Magnolia would help put me at ease. I could use another ally. And Lauren remembered growing up here, maybe she could help me jog loose all these blocked memories.

If I really wanted another chance, I had to give it to others, too. There was one thing really holding me back, though. Something I had to know before I took another step forward.

"Can you answer one question for me before we go?"

Lauren turned to face me, her eyes serious.

"I've never slept with any of my patients, Simone. It's highly unprofessional and diminishes my hard work."

Whoa. She'd known just what I was going to ask. And she hadn't answered me defensively or dismissed why it was so important to me. If she was going to extend that grace to me, I'd sure give it back to her.

"Cool," I said. "Then let's go have a drink."

CHAPTER NINETEEN

"On a Friday night, you can't find a single table here." Lauren's ponytail bobbed with each step she took into Gino's Pizzeria. Nostalgia greeted me at the door, almost as strong as the mouthwatering scent of wood-fired pizza. My stomach grumbled. As far as I was concerned, there was little on this planet that melted cheese and doughy bread couldn't solve.

"Luckily for us, it's Tuesday." I followed her to the small booth in the corner. All the locals knew it was *the* spot. Not too close to the bathrooms, in Gino's eyeline so he didn't forget your order, and close enough to an overhead vent to always be the right temperature.

And, while Gino kept a close eye on the spot, he often got busy on weekends. This was the spot where young couples went when they wanted to—ahem—not keep their hands to themselves.

"Home sweet home." Lauren giggled and plopped into her chair. "Ethan and I have a lot of happy memories of this spot. We even got divorced here."

"Nice that it's a happy memory for you." I slid into the other side, ignoring the choke of my throat. "I don't know that it will be for me when I get divorced."

"Oh gosh, I'm sorry, Simone." Lauren bit down on her lower lip almost hard enough to draw blood. "I didn't mean to sound so cavalier about it."

"It's fine, Lauren." I waved at the strange old lady I'd seen talking to the Mighty Oak the other day. She was with another woman, about my age, whom I didn't recognize and a third person I could only describe as a goddess. Given what I'd learned, my guess was that she was an actual goddess. I drew my attention back to Lauren.

"You don't have to choose your words so carefully around me. Trust me, I'm a blurter, too."

"Thank you." She threaded her ponytail through her fingers with a furrowed brow. "I'm always so self-aware, and yet I still manage to say dumb shit."

"Join the club."

A waitress swung by, greeting us by name although I didn't recognize her. Small towns, I suppose. Word traveled fast. Then again, I'd grown up here. Maybe I knew her and didn't remember.

"Dammit." I hadn't meant to say it out loud. Lauren and the waitress turned to me in unison. "Ignore me, I'm just in my head."

After the waitress left, Lauren angled her body to face me. We were so close in the booth our knees were touching. That was the beauty of this corner. You couldn't escape whomever you were with. An interesting, but ultimately terrifying, thought pinged my brain.

"Did you put us here to hit on me?" Lauren's laugh drew stares from everyone around us. A flush of embarrassment heated my cheeks and neck. "So ... no."

"I'm sorry again, Simone." Lauren dabbed at the tears in her eyes with a napkin akin to sandpaper. "You just looked so scared."

"Well, it's not because you aren't hot," I offered. "And I've played around with the idea before. I'm just ... not ready for that. Romance, I mean. Of any kind."

"You're safe, friend." Lauren patted my hand, and when I relaxed, I wasn't sure if it was because of her light touch or the use of the word friend. I'd already counted my lucky stars that I'd found Brianne. Was another friendship even possible? Especially with someone who hadn't been particularly nice to me way back when?

"I'm so damn self-conscious all the time, Lauren." I accepted the cold beer the waitress put in front of me with a smile. "Everyone is judging and waiting on me to either fail or pass. And I feel like Agatha is watching me. All the time."

"In her own way, she is." Lauren said. She broke a piece of bread out of the basket set in front of us, handing half to me. "What do you remember about her?"

"That she was imposing. Old even when I was a little girl. And passionate." I broke it apart, chewing as I dipped into my memories. "It's all still a bit hazy, but the impression in my brain is that she really, really loved what she did. And cared about improving people."

"That was her. She had high expectations because she met them herself." Lauren swiped her napkin across her lips and leaned back to face me. "I came to her with my grand notion of a wellness center that featured therapy fresh out of college. I was barely an adult, but she treated me like an equal.

"Even then, she made me feel so seen and validated." She fiddled with her bread before setting it back down. I couldn't fathom saying no to bread. "As we became colleagues, and eventually partners, she never shot down any crazy idea I had."

"Like fae giving pedicures and facials in the same building a nymph is being treated for PTSD?" I washed down the bread with more beer, feeling a bit like my neanderthal ancestors. Pain, bad. Bread, good. Beer, better. Of course, the conversation we were having was way more than basic.

"Exactly." A salad I hadn't heard Lauren order arrived with two plates. Lauren split it without asking, handing mine to me as her story unfolded. "For a while, it was just the two of us. But I saw so much room for growth. Every time I brought it up, she'd tell me I was part of a bigger plan."

"That plan included me." The bread lodged in my throat, unwilling to go down. Luckily, I had beer. "And Brianne. I think we were supposed to start at the same time. Everything was supposed to be put into motion then."

"Twenty years ago," Lauren said, nodding in confirmation. "It's when the Twins started, too."

For a moment, the room disappeared. Lauren squinted at me as if I were disappearing from the end of a long tunnel. It was almost like my skeletal system was vibrating. My bones rattled inside me, churning something deep in my roots. I tried to let myself breathe, to let whatever it was that was begging to come to the surface arise on its own.

That damn memory. That damn crucial memory, edging me along

but never letting me experience release. I squeezed my eyes shut. Reaching for it. The answer was right there. Why couldn't I access it?

A loud crash jolted me back to the table. My head flung backwards, slamming against the high back of our booth. Blinking through tears, the restaurant came back into focus.

A large man with a grease-stained white tee crowded the table in front of us. A few straggly strands of hair combed over one side of his balding head. His eyes were near invisible under bushy eyebrows, a deeper shade of red than the pepperoni on the pizza he'd just dropped.

But the kind of smile that makes you feel all warm inside stretched wide across his freckled face.

"Well, there you are, girl! I heard you were in town and wondered when you'd find your way to me." He ignored the waitress clamoring at his feet to clean the mess he'd made. With arms stretched out wide, he beckoned me forward. "Get over here and give me a hug."

"Hey, Gino. It's sure good to see you." I'd said it to be polite. Not because it wasn't good to see him, but because my memory of him was just as dim as the lighting. With a sheepish grin at Lauren, I obeyed his order. He wrapped me in a hug warmer than fleece, holding me so close I could barely breathe.

But the scent of him, yeast and sweat and deodorant, was more familiar than I realized. And the longer he held me, the crisper my past. Holy cow. I'd worked here. I'd been the waitress shyly taking orders while Lauren and Ethan, or one of her ilk, sucked face in the corner booth.

And I'd loved it here. Sure, the floor was sticky, and the tips were lousy, but it had been fun. Chatting with locals. Sneaking breadsticks at breaktime. Bullshitting with Gino, who acted like the loud uncle at holiday dinners.

Gino and I exchanged a brief catch up, and I promised to come back more often and visit.

"We're all rooting for ya, kid." He gave me a punch on the shoulder that should have been light but wasn't, then hurried off with a wink.

"Did you remember that I used to work here?" I asked Lauren, rubbing my shoulder and returning to my seat. I nodded thanks to the waitress as she brought us a fresh pizza.

"Yeah." She served me again, passing my slice on a plate before taking her own. "I mean, sort of. Ethan reminded me, on Agatha's last day." A slight blush lit her cheeks. "It was such a strange night, with her insisting on that last-minute change to her will. He came over, and we talked."

"He came over close to midnight?" I gave her a sly wink, pretending jealousy wasn't crawling around inside me like a damn feral raccoon. "You sure you two are just friends?"

The blush deepened, spreading down her cheeks and onto her neck.

"I'm sure. I always have been, to be honest. I just don't get ... feelings like that for other people." She looked at her pizza as if it were the most interesting thing in the world. "I pushed it down in high school. You know"—she glanced up at me—"because I was the head cheerleader and popular. Ethan and I were expected to date. I hated it. It's part of why I was so mean. I was fighting so hard to keep all these things I really didn't want."

It was at that moment that I realized how similar Lauren and I were. I'd always envisioned her as higher than me. Somehow better because she was taller and more graceful and seemed to have it all together. I assumed her casual cruelty in high school was part of her personality. I'd never even hated her for it, though.

"I get it." I reached across the table and squeezed her hand. "Apparently, I've done a lot of that, too."

"Anyway"—the blush disappeared and Lauren's sunshine returned —"once I started with Agatha and slid into my power, the past just sort of dissipated. Ethan and I were both relieved when we divorced. Our friendship was always more natural than our romance."

"I don't know that I ever called Jeff my friend. We'd been part of the same group in college, pals in the sense that we were always at the same bar or parties. But friends?" I bit into the pizza, taking a moment to relish the ooze of it on my tongue. "Nope. It went straight from 'I know that guy' to 'I'm dating that guy' to 'I'm married to that guy' once I got pregnant."

"He wasn't right for you." Lauren, sinking into our new gal pal dynamic, inhaled her pizza. I grabbed another slice and dropped it on her plate before loading my own. Like I said, there's not much in this world that can't be fixed with good food. "There's someone else out there."

There might have been a catch in her voice. I couldn't quite grab it, and I wasn't sure I wanted to. We ate in silence, enjoying the ambience of Gino's pizzeria, even on a Tuesday. I drank more beer.

"I hope it happens for Ethan." Lauren sat back with a happy sigh, dropping her napkin to her plate. "He still hasn't met his fated mate. Keeps marrying women clearly not right for him."

"Fated mate?" The words had been uttered so casually; I wasn't shocked when Lauren looked at me like I had broccoli coming out of my ears.

"Yeah, you know." Her eyebrows disappeared behind her bangs. "His destined soulmate."

"No idea what you're talking about," I said into my beer. Whatever Lauren was saying, I was not getting it.

"Ethan is a wolf shifter, Simone." Lauren shook her head, taking a dainty sip of her wine. "I assumed he told you in high school?"

I set my beer down, staring into it like I was reading tea leaves. Had he mentioned it in high school? I didn't think so. He'd expressed frustration that I ran faster than him. We'd joked about physical fitness levels.

He definitely had not mentioned being a wolf shifter.

"Ethan Mosely," I murmured. "Leading the Pack in Louisiana Justice."

"His stupid personal injury slogan." Beside me, Lauren scoffed. "I told him it was a bit on the nose."

"I've seen a wolf around town." My stomach churned again. I stopped and swallowed. I was not going to throw up all of that wonderful pizza and beer. "It seems like it's ... guarding me."

Lauren tilted her head and scowled, but she didn't speak.

"Long, dark fur. Hauntingly familiar eyes." Even as I said it, I knew it wasn't Ethan. "Not Ethan. Now that I think about it, it's definitely not him. Still, I can't shake the feeling that I know the wolf."

Whatever Lauren was thinking about, she didn't let it show. The scowl cleared, and her lovely face blanked. Wow. Was that a witch thing? I couldn't read a single emotion off her.

She sipped her wine, watching me work things out. But the tension that grew between us, and this new info about Ethan I needed to digest, threw me off guard.

"If I were a better witch, I think I could force you to tell me what I'm missing." I'd meant it to come out lighthearted, but there was an undertone to my voice I didn't recognize. Like I was testing the waters with a threat I didn't intend to fulfill. "Couldn't I?"

"As Ephemeral Supreme, Simone, you could direct me to tell you anything you needed to know." Resentment coated her words like icy slime. "Assuming I knew the answers."

Oof. I wanted to shrink in my chair. I'd touched a nerve.

"I'm so tired, Lauren." It was true, and it had come out without me thinking about it. The panic attack earlier in the day, my attempt to learn magic, all this new information, and a belly full of beer and pizza finally all landed on me like a leaded door.

I didn't want more tension with Lauren. I didn't want her to hate me. I just wanted to go back to the house and sleep.

"I'm not interested in forcing you to do anything. I want and need you on my side." I finished the last of my beer, fishing for cash from my wallet to leave on the table. "I'm here because you said you wanted to talk. Just tell me what you need to say, and we can call it a night. You're not my enemy, and you never will be."

In the same moment my throat relaxed, Lauren's shoulders dropped. Her usual chipper smile returned to her face, lighting her pretty blue eyes.

"Your money's no good here." She shoved my cash back at me and set her credit card on the table. It had the business name on it. This was technically still a business dinner. That was smart of her. I had a lot to learn.

After the waitress left, Lauren propped her elbows on the table and focused on me.

"I wanted to apologize for the way I treated you in high school. In particular, the day I screwed everything up." For a moment, her lower lip trembled. She chewed on it until it stilled. "I was hurt and jealous. I wanted you to be, too."

The waitress returned with the bill, giving me time to dig into my memory. Ethan had mentioned this, too. Something happened between us senior year.

Whatever it was, I didn't remember. And I clearly wasn't ready to.

"I forgive you, Lauren. I'd like us to be friends. Start fresh and build Magnolia Wellness into something even greater than it is now."

"I'd like that too, Simone." Her smile was one of pure relief.

We rose together. My words were slurred enough that I questioned how many beers I'd drunk. But as we walked out, it wasn't drunkenness that made my legs wobble and threw my balance off.

It was a deep-rooted fatigue. I was spent. I could not handle any more.

We said goodbye, and I stumbled home, trying to analyze what I was feeling. Mostly, clouded. Caught between the supernatural and what Ethan had called the mundane. I wanted to try and do everything I could to succeed at the Magnolia. I also wanted to go back to the life I was pretending still existed in New Orleans.

I didn't feel capable of doing either.

I reached the back door to the Magnolia and climbed up the stairs. My hand was on the doorknob when the hair on my arm stood on end. I peered over the balcony, squinting at shadows in the fenced-in gardens. One of them moved.

The wolf stepped into a patch of light, meeting my eyes. I opened my mouth to speak. Found I had very little to say.

"I'm too tired to do this with you right now," I told the wolf. Without waiting for a reply, I went inside and collapsed on the bed I now called mine.

CHAPTER TWENTY

By Friday, part of me regretted accepting Brianne's dinner invitation. I wanted to spend time with her outside the office, but my to-the-bone weariness refused to release its grip. For all my resolve to try and make the best of things, I still held back. A slew of canceled appointments hadn't helped. And the patients who did show up got a distant, struggling version of me.

I'd managed a few more purposeful feats of magic during the week, and I clung to that lifeline as I left the house. It now sported fresh paint the color of a rising sun in winter, with green and ivory accents, as if it were a magnolia itself. The shutters were secured to the house, rather than balancing on rusty nails. And the flower beds, though bare, were packed with fresh soil and primed to bloom whatever House planted.

It was progress. Not enough, but a step in the right direction.

Brianne lived in a quaint suburban house on the edges of town. A pretty white porch stretched across the front of the house, with stairs leading up to the inviting red door directly in the center. Oversized windows on each side beckoned visitors into domestic heaven.

The two-story home was painted a deep shade of blue. Kids' toys were scattered along the porch. Tiny, adorable pairs of glittery pink sandals graced the doormat. A second pair of larger tennis shoes rested on the rocker, as if they'd been thrown there on the way inside.

Before I had a chance to ring the bell, Brianne opened the door, welcoming me amidst the chaos of high-pitch squeals and laughter behind her.

"Sorry for the noise." She hugged me close in the doorway, cooing over the bottle of wine I'd remembered at the last moment to bring. Well, House remembered and had it on a table by the door when I was leaving. "Nate got home late. The kids are over-excited to see him. Come in and meet the fam."

I followed her inside, smiling at the heartwarming image her home created. Comfortably messy, with bold colors and mismatched furniture. Two kids, a girl no more than five and a boy I'd put around fifteen, wrestled their father as he wiggled and twisted to reach their best tickle spots. It was wholesome to witness, particularly as kids the boy's age tended to be sullen and withdrawn.

I rubbed at the space in my heart where my pain over Gabe lived. Brianne bumped my shoulder, almost as if she knew what I was thinking.

"All right, you animals, my new friend is here. Get off your dad and come meet Simone."

With no small amount of reluctance, they crawled off their father's back and trudged over obediently.

"Hey. I'm Nolan." At fifteen, Brianne's boy towered over her. Yet he stood behind her as if she could protect him from the world. Thin lips lifted into a crooked smile. His mama's smile. "Nice to meet you."

"You too, Nolan." His awkward shyness was adorable, and I wondered if he realized what a handsome young man he was. His fair skin was pimple-free. Jet black hair flopped around on his head, and his small but intensely blue eyes gave you the feeling of being truly seen. He had the look of a high school heartthrob, and his shy aura likely made the teens swoon.

As soon as I acknowledged him, he disappeared, as if the mere act of introducing himself had taken all his effort. His sister, on the other hand, pushed right past her parents and marched over to me. She extended her hand to shake mine, and I knew immediately I was going to become this girl's new aunt. Or snack bitch. Whatever she allowed.

"Hello, Miss Simone. I'm Natalie." Her hair was a jumbled mess of blond knots landing below her round, adorable face. Large, curious eyes the same bright emerald shade as her mother's looked up at me with unnerving wisdom. This little girl was five going on eighty-five.

"Nice to meet you, Natalie. I'm Simone." I shook her tiny hand. "I love your nail polish."

"Thank you." Her voice held an air of approval. I'd passed a test by commenting on the pink glitter adorning her fingers. "They match daddy's."

"It looks better on you, Kitten." Brianne's husband strolled forward on long, slender legs. He laced one arm around his wife, pulling her close. He extended the other to display his sparkling, pointed nails. I barely saw them.

Longish dark hair danced at the edge of his collar. Pale, flawless skin almost shined under the dark sweater and jeans he wore on his long, lanky frame. He smiled at me. It was a welcoming smile, not-at-all menacing.

Yet a chill ran up my spine. His grin exposed extended canines, each scalpel-sharp.

"Nice to finally meet you, Simone. I'm Nate Steele."

His hand was ice cold. His voice was syrup and honey.

Holy cannoli. Brianne's doting husband was a vampire.

I gulped. I literally gulped.

"Brianne's spoken a lot about your latest life changes." Nate continued like I wasn't standing there with my mouth hanging open. "I must say, I admire your ability to take on something so massive with such grace."

"Oh, I don't know that I've been the least bit graceful." A woman could get lost in eyes like that. Everything I knew about vampires was lore or from bad movies. Here was one, in the scary-ass flesh, complimenting me on a grace I didn't possess after wrestling with his half-human kids.

I couldn't stop staring. Oh God, was he possessing me with those piercing blue eyes? Did vampires possess? No, it was called something else.

Enthralled. Was he enthralling me? Did I feel enthralled?

No. The only thing I felt was stupid. Brianne and her husband had welcomed me into their home, and I was gaping at him like he was in a zoo. I closed my mouth.

"Definitely not handling anything with grace," I repeated, wiping drool off my lip. "But I'm trying to adapt."

"Which is a form of grace itself." He released my hand and planted a soft kiss on Brianne's cheek. "The hellions and I are going to clean up for dinner. Then we're setting the table so you two can talk."

At the kids' twin groans, he sent them a look that rooted me to the spot. Damn, he was scary. To me.

Natalie stuck her tongue out with a wicked giggle, and his menace turned to mirth in the blink of an eye. With a vicious, fake hiss, he scooped her up and over his shoulder. Her shriek tensed every inch of my body. Nolan emitted a warrior's whoop and, brandishing a fake sword, chased after them.

"Mayhem." Brianne shook her head as if the scene had been totally normal. Which, I suppose to her, it had. "Thank you for the wine."

"It's, uh, red." I shrugged my shoulders.

"Our favorite." Brianne turned toward the kitchen. My feet followed. "I probably should have told you. You know, about Nate. But I thought seeing the look on your face would be hilarious." She popped the cork and poured three tall glasses. I watched the swirling liquid in a daze as she handed me one. "Gotta admit, I was right."

"House chose the wine for me. I see it shares your sense of humor."

Brianne's head tipped back. When she laughed, I was surprised to find I was able to join in.

Dinner was a surreal collage of idle chatter and hearty foods. Nate sipped his wine and spooned another liquid from a wide bowl. I didn't want to think about what it was or where it came from.

"Eat your broccoli, darling, not just your blood." Brianne nudged Nolan's plate closer, stabbing a stalk with a fork and waving it at him when his face dropped into a grimace. "It won't go away just because you don't like it."

"One day it will," he mumbled. I couldn't quite suppress the shudder that blanketed me.

"So." I finished a bite of the lightly fried fish Nate had cooked perfectly. "How did you two meet?"

"We worked together back in Atlanta." Nate slid his hand over Brianne's, his eyes shining. "She was the best accountant at the bank, and I was the head of finance. Her boss and four times her age. It was wildly inappropriate."

For a moment, they gazed at one another as if they were the only ones in the room. Natalie sighed dreamily while Nolan made gagging noises—their parents clearly did this often.

"Brianne, you have an accounting background?" I asked. "I thought you were managing the Magnolia."

"I do. And I am." Brianne pulled her attention away from her husband. "I do the basic bookkeeping for the Magnolia, but I'm not using my degree to its full extent."

There was an interesting wistfulness to her voice, like she wanted to do more. I still hadn't given much thought to the business of the Magnolia. It seemed like wasted effort, particularly if I couldn't keep the therapy practice going. Eventually, if I managed to become Supreme, I'd want to know more. But in the meantime, I was letting the place run itself.

Or, it seemed, I was letting Brianne run the place. Which my gut told me was just fine. For now.

"Atlanta, huh?" I wrenched myself away from my internal monologue. "Isn't it sunny there?"

"It is. But by the grace of the universe, I don't burn to ash in daylight." Nate propped his chin on his hands and batted his eyes my way. "I glitter like a million diamonds."

"You do not." Brianne nudged him, and Natalie giggled. "Most of what you know about vampires is lore, Simone. As you can see, they are really quite domesticated."

"How dare you imply I'm domesticated." Nate made a play for Brianne's neck, nuzzling in as if he might bite before planting a noisy kiss. She pushed him away, her cheeks flushing a deep red.

The way they adored each other was like a sharp knife to my heart. Someone had looked at me that way once. Someone had stroked my hair and spoken with so much tenderness it was like he held the whole of his emotions for me in his voice.

Someone had left me so flushed with desire it bloomed on my body.

It hadn't been Jeff. My thoughts escaped to that summer after high school, and the man who'd disappeared into the night, taking my heart with him.

I was happy for Brianne. She deserved a home and family full of love and respect. The playfulness they all had spoke of a deeper affection. As they ate and we chatted, their familial bond showed. They were a team. A well-oiled machine with few squeaky wheels. A perfect blend of magic and mundane.

I'd never seen anything like it. As I poked at dessert, I realized this was the reason Brianne invited me to dinner. So that I could see that the supernatural aspect of them was another aspect of their personalities.

This could have been any house with any family. This one just happened to have a vampire living there. And the sooner I embraced that, the better able I'd be to help them.

Which would mean embracing my own supernatural abilities as well, a feat I couldn't imagine overcoming without facing up to the past I was so desperate to avoid.

CHAPTER TWENTY-ONE

"My dear, do you play poker?" Nate rose and stacked the dishes, passing them to Nolan. With a false grumble, he took them into the kitchen. Natalie rounded the table to stack utensils while Nate refilled my wine glass.

"Not really," I answered. "I don't think I'd be very good at it."

"Definitely not." He clinked his glass to mine in cheers. "You have a most expressive face."

It was my turn to blush. I already knew I wore my emotions like a sleeve.

"I'm sorry, Nate." I stood with Brianne, holding tight to the wine. House had excellent taste. It was delicious. "I don't mean to be rude. I'm ... in my head a lot these days. Figuring life out, I guess."

"My dear, what is life if not a mystery never to be solved?" He looped his arm in mine, guiding me to the front door. We'd barely finished dinner, and I was being kicked out. Had I been more rude than I realized? "If I've learned anything in my two-hundred years on this planet, it's that I know nothing."

He wasn't kicking me out. Instead, he guided me to the front porch, gesturing for me to take a seat on one of the cushioned, white rockers. He took the opposite chair, patting his lap and motioning to his wife.

"It's okay not to have all the answers, Simone. But you should know you're in a safe place." Brianne slid onto his lap and nuzzled close to his chest. "We moved to Treater's Way to raise our children in an environment where they could be themselves. Where we wouldn't have to hide the aspects that make them so unique and wonderful."

"Like their half-human side," Nate added with a chuckle.

The neighborhood was quiet. Families were likely all settled down for the evening, finishing homework or watching television. This could have been any suburban neighborhood, not unlike the one I'd grown up in. My thoughts drifted back to the boy and his maybe Cerberus I'd seen at my old house. How many of these seemingly normal families included something or someone paranormal?

Happy families, living their lives just like any family in any town. The exact thing I'd wanted for myself and lost by my own choice.

Tears stung my eyes then flowed down my cheeks before I could stop them.

"I'm so sorry." I sobbed the words out. "This is a wine-induced drama moment."

Nate and Brianne did that thing close couples do. With a single look, they held an entire conversation. They stood up so Nate could leave. He placed a soothing hand on my shoulder and squeezed on his way inside.

Brianne let me sob quietly for a moment longer. Well, in my mind it was quiet. In reality, I was choking and gulping like a pug after a good sneeze.

"Give me the drama." Brianne leaned forward and focused on me. "What's holding you back, Simone?"

I shook my head, burying my face in my hands. I wanted to sink into the porch and slither away. Everything was brewing inside me, rumbling around like I'd drunk a dozen cups of old, strong coffee. I was nasty inside. Full of gunk and guilt and unease.

"I don't know if I'm worth all of this." I sniffed and grabbed for my wine, desperate to coat my tongue with something other than bitter self-pity. "I think maybe Agatha made a terrible mistake basing her inheritance on who I might have become thirty years ago, rather than who I am today."

Brianne didn't reply. She watched me, somehow understanding I didn't want placating. I needed to process everything I had kept pushed down. Now that I understood my words had power, something told me that saying the ugly part out loud would actually help me to heal. The thing was ...

"I don't deserve to heal. Deep down, I'm too ashamed of the choices I've made to move forward."

Brianne's sharp inhale forced me to open my eyes. Out of the corners, I could make out a strange orange glow. When I turned toward the glow, it escaped. I turned left and right in my chair, trying to catch it. But each time, it was just out of reach.

"It's all around you, Sweets." Brianne's voice was heavy with a compassion I didn't feel I deserved. "Tell me why you feel that you don't deserve to heal."

She would have made a great therapist. Repeating my words to me was a classic technique. The way she made people feel seen and validated ...

It reminded me of my mother. Of the unwavering support she'd had for me before she died.

"I always dreamed of being the kind of mother that my mama was," I managed to choke out. "And, clearly, the kind of mother you are. The kind who lets their child grow and be themselves."

I drew my breath in deep. It was too ugly to hold in. Too ugly to let out. But it wasn't giving me a choice.

"I failed my son, Brianne. I failed Gabe at every turn. Now, he won't even talk to me. And I don't blame him one bit."

God, the heaving sobs returned. I hiccupped and shuddered. Tears and snot raced down my face. Brianne went inside, returning with a cool washcloth and tissues. She sat and drank her wine, letting all my ugly ooze out.

It was strange—unexpected, really. Like lancing a boil or sucking venom from a wound. There wasn't anything Brianne could say to make me feel better. But her presence was all I needed to clear out the infection of my own making.

Having somewhere safe to be as raw and ugly as I needed to be. As a therapist, I should have understood that. After all, it was what I was supposed to do for my clients. It was what I had wanted for my son.

"Tell me about Gabe, Simone."

At last, the waterfall slowed to a trickle. I blew my nose and wiped my face clean.

"He was a delightfully quirky kid," I said. "Artistic and strange in all the best ways. He always asked questions, and sometimes they were insightful and other times they were just weird. One time, we saw this woman in a store. She was wearing too much perfume to cover up body odor. The smell was intense. Neither of us said anything, of course."

I paused to laugh and take a shaky sip of wine.

"But when we got to the car, Gabe asked me if he was supposed to see squiggly lines around people when they smelled bad. He hadn't seen any when we passed that woman, and he thought that meant something was wrong with his eyesight."

"He sounds like an artist," Brianne said with a chuckle.

"He is. Or he wanted to be. Jeff and I convinced him that graphic design was a more practical use of his talent." I bit my lip to keep it from trembling. "I think we squashed some of his ambition without meaning to."

"Is that why he's not talking to you?" I wanted to damn Brianne for asking that question. I couldn't stop crying. I pressed the washcloth to my face.

"No. We weren't close, but we had a decent relationship," I responded. "But a few weeks ago, when I walked in on Jeff ..."

I didn't want to relive that day. But Brianne waited. I told her the details, what I could remember. A meeting with Agatha that was still a blur in my head. Rushing home with a pounding headache. Finding him in bed with his physical therapist. Throwing up on her shoes.

"I ran out, driving around for hours with the music too loud and the windows open even though it was hot. When I ran out of gas, I pulled into a crappy station near my office. It was almost midnight by then."

I paused again, drawing in breath, preparing myself. Sometimes, you just gotta dive into the ugly part.

"I was alone and angry and realized I didn't have a single friend I could call. So, I called Gabe. He's in California, two hours behind us. It was Friday night, he's a college kid, so of course he was at a party." Another sob escaped. I let it. "But he still answered the phone like he'd been expecting me.

"I said horrible things about Jeff to him. Things a son doesn't deserve to know about his father, no matter what his father's done." I leaned forward, certain I was about to heave. A cool washcloth landed on my neck. "And he got upset, which he had every right to be. Then I ..."

My voice trailed. Let the ugly out, Simone.

"I told him he was obviously going to choose his father because he was just like him."

"Oh, honey." There was criticism laced in Brianne's voice. I couldn't blame her. "Did he respond?"

"I didn't give him a chance to." I stood up and paced the porch, no longer able to keep still. Plus, when I threw up, I wanted it to be in the nearby bushes and not all over her pretty stained wood. "I told him to forget I ever existed because he was better off alone than with a mother who constantly screwed up."

I hadn't even finished speaking when the realization hit—I'd screwed things up with Gabe. Just like Jeff, my words had hexed him. No wonder he hadn't returned any of my calls or texts.

He didn't know who I was anymore.

Brianne rushed to grab me when my knees went weak. She didn't need to, though, because I'd grabbed the railing. All the contents of that lovely wine and delicious dinner disappeared into the darkness of the lawn.

No wonder I had held my past at bay. Facing it meant facing the deepest, darkest shadows in my own soul.

How could a single mistake prove so fatal? How could I ever fix something so horrible?

What other secrets was I keeping buried?

CHAPTER TWENTY-TWO

Brianne urged me to stay the night, but I insisted on walking home. I wanted a shower and the bedroom that seemed to be my only sanctuary at the moment. I had a lot to atone for, even more to think about, and a deep, ugly fact to face.

By constantly squashing my power and ignoring my voice, I'd done more than hurt myself or hold myself back. My inability to embrace my powers was affecting others. I'd alienated my son, the one person I loved most in the world. I'd hurt Jeff and Doug, and even if it was unintentional, I needed to be more responsible.

I had a lot to fix. Maybe *I* didn't deserve everything Agatha had left me or to be forgiven, but no one else should suffer for my own lack of self-worth.

The exterior lights accenting the path to the Magnolia were brighter as I neared. I hadn't done that. There were wild purple flowers I didn't recognize blooming in the window boxes. The two rockers on the porch had fresh paint in the same shade. I hadn't done that either.

But, I'd given House a nudge. And it made her stronger.

"You're looking more beautiful every day, House, did you know that?"

If a house could preen, that's what happened. There was a shimmer, so slight I almost didn't catch it, and an even slighter vibration beneath my feet. The windowpanes, only moments ago buried under a layer of grime, wiped themselves clean.

"Oh, that's lovely, House!"

There was another preen. I rounded the front of the house and made my way down the narrow pathway—barely wide enough for one person—to the metal stairs in the back leading to my apartment. Even in the dim of night, I could see they'd been redone, too.

"You're starting to blossom. Just like a magnolia, you sweet Magnolia." I touched my hand to the wall, a friendly pat on the side.

The response was chaos.

Vivid lights flashed red, blinding me. An ear-piercing wail shrieked through the silence until my eardrums ached. In a fit of terror, I darted toward my stairs, my heart pounding in my chest. Had I set off an alarm? Brianne hadn't mentioned anything about one.

I stopped just short of the stairs.

My wolf—and I considered him mine whether he wanted to be or not—guarded the back entrance to the Magnolia. By now, I had no reason to believe he would hurt me. And since I'd learned Ethan was a wolf shifter, I had to assume I was dealing with someone who was also part-human.

Given the way every inch of my body responded to the slightest twitch of his fur, I'd venture a guess this was someone I knew. And who knew me.

"Whoever you are, I'm sorry but I don't remember you." My throat wavered, a sign I was lying to myself. "Okay, I remember you, and there's an obvious connection here, but I can't find it yet." I waved my hand around my head. "I'm having memory issues."

I was talking to a wolf in the dark, protecting a magic house I'd just inherited. Life got a little stranger each day. The wolf stepped forward, tilting his head toward the floodlights to make himself more visible. It was the first time I noticed he wore a collar.

Attached to the collar was a charm with a familiar logo. Lone Wolf Sentries. The same security firm where Doug worked.

"So, I tripped an alarm and security responded. Sorry. Not sure how I did that." Not Ethan, but this wolf was not Doug either, who'd had nothing in his files about being part dog. "Can you ... show yourself to me? I'd love to know who you are."

Hoo boy, the way that flowed from my body was like water flowing through a stream. Crystal clear in a way that left me tingly. Yes, please, Mr. Wolfy. Show me who you are.

The wolf's ears rotated forward. He let out a single sharp bark.

"Are you not allowed to ... shift on duty?"

He took another step forward. As he did, the air between us shimmered. A thousand particles of light illuminated the yard. He was a haze on all fours, then nearly on two.

"Hey, CC, sorry about that!" Gumbo hopped from the balcony above to land in front of me. In a blink, the wolf was back on the pads of his paws. And a surprisingly horny thrill landed in my gut like a thud.

I had a wolf kink. Who knew?

"Brianne called to tell me you were on your way." Gumbo licked one orange-nailed paw, giving me time to digest that he had a phone. "I was supposed to greet you before you got here, to keep the alarm from going off. But you took too long, and I fell asleep."

"I took the long route home, I guess." My eyes were on the wolf, trying to read the expression in his eyes. Before I could figure it out, he bounded off to the trees lining the back of the property and disappeared. "Why hasn't the alarm gone off before?"

"There's always been someone who belonged here." Gumbo padded up the stairs. "I'll let you in."

I followed him in and rushed to the shower. Cold sweat covered my skin. I was raw from dinner. Heartbroken about my son. And filled with wolf-induced adrenaline.

But most of all, a profound sense of disappointment shrouded me. The alarm had gone off because I still didn't belong. I was still an outsider.

That night, my dreams were tormented and frenetic. Moments from my life flashed through my mind in a chaotic montage. A reserved smile at Jeff on our wedding day. Intense studying in the college library. Laughing with Ethan as we ran the high school track. Visiting Agatha here at a different but still familiar Magnolia. That damn park bench that teased me with its importance yet refused to show.

The wolf was there, in every image, lurking in corners and hiding in bushes. His green eyes, intense and longing, followed my every move. I searched for him, desperate for the feel of him, wanting nothing more than to get lost in him.

But he was always just out of reach, the very thing I longed for and could never have, a bittersweet desire forever unfulfilled, leaving me intoxicated and alone.

CHAPTER TWENTY-THREE

I bandied about the house most of Saturday, watching junk TV and going through the photo albums I'd found in the chest underneath the Blue Hoard.

I was restless and needed action. I'd been far too passive the last few weeks, ever since I'd walked in on Jeff with his hand in the metaphorical cookie jar. Sure, in fits and starts I'd made progress, but it was always two steps forward and three steps back.

One thing I knew with absolute certainty was that I needed to restore my memories and become more intentional with my witchcraft. I spent thirty minutes staring at myself in the bathroom mirror, willing my memories to return. No matter what I said, they remained hidden. I couldn't pull that sensation of deep truth that I'd used to restore parts of the house. I couldn't even access the anger and hurt that led to Jeff's curses. Or my own son forgetting me.

Overwhelm was the only tangible emotion inside me. It ate at me, a thousand tiny mice racing around the maze of my brain searching for cheese. I prowled the living room like my wolf, anxious and unsteady. I plopped down on the red couch, flipping through television I didn't even see before turning it off with a huff.

It seemed silly. My own miracle question had been answered with a true miracle. The irony of that was not lost on me. A thriving business had been dumped in my lap in a place I'd once called home. Maybe work would help alleviate this restlessness.

"I need an office, House. I should make lists and get organized. I can't keep it all up here anymore." I slapped the side of my head. "Can you help me?"

A creaking sound at the end of the hallway roused me to my feet. Of course, there was already an office opposite my bedroom. I'd opened the door the first day I arrived then forgotten all about it.

But the office I stood in now was different. Massive windows covered the front wall, overlooking the entrance to the Magnolia. The tree-lined street with its charming houses-turned-businesses made me smile. I couldn't quite see Illusion Square from my view, but the tops of the Mighty Oak assured me it was nearby.

I'd missed this in New Orleans. The sense of community that a small town brings. My crappy office in a crappy shopping center was the opposite of soothing. Who wanted to get therapy next to a pawn shop and fast-food joint?

Surveying the office, I realized it was the very one I'd seen on a home improvement show earlier in the day, decorated in something the host called barnyard chic. A robin's egg blue desk faced the windows from the opposite end of the office. Behind it were tall shelves with recessed spaces that matched the desk. Flowers and vases sparsely populated the shelves.

Gumbo was already asleep on the bright pink chair in the corner. His nails and bow matched its happy hue. He opened his eyes a slit when I scratched behind his ear. With a purr, he drifted off. Soft music drifted from a speaker/charger on the table where my phone somehow had appeared.

I took my seat. It was wide and comfy, a soft cream color with leather like butter. A Bayou Bliss popped into existence on a ceramic coaster. I opened a drawer to find a stack of legal pads and pens.

"Thanks, House. Let's get started."

Business stuff was easier to process, so I began with that. If I was staying, I'd need to cancel my lease on my other office. I was fairly certain everything I wanted to keep from my home with Jeff was already here, but I would want to verify that with my own eyes. I'd need to dissolve my corporation, or have it legally merged into the Magnolia. I'd need—and my hand hovered before I wrote it—a divorce.

If I wasn't staying, I'd need to formally resign my position here. I'd want a new place with a new lease, and I'd want to move my office

Uptown, which meant a small business loan I probably couldn't get. Maybe I would find a place like this Uptown or in the Garden District, granted without the magical element, and live on the top floor. That might cut down on expenses.

Either way, I was getting a divorce, which meant finding a lawyer. Jeff and I had a family lawyer, but he was a buddy from college, and I didn't want to use someone who would show bias. Ethan seemed like the logical step.

My list drifted to the Magnolia. Succeeding as a therapist here meant resolving things with Doug. Whatever I'd done to him, the town was on his side. I may never have friendships with the Twins, but I'd have to find a way to work with them.

Both of those meant harnessing my power. I wanted to learn more about what it meant to be a word witch beyond the surface stuff I already did. Did I need to practice spells? Practice chants? Make charm bags or work with herbs?

I shuddered at the thought. If I had to garden, I would be screwed. Hopefully, I could find what I needed at the apothecary in Illusion Square. Or rely on House. I added helping House regain its full strength to my list. Was there a way to do that while still ephemeral?

I stumbled over the word as I wrote it. Ephemeral. Temporary. A reminder that I still didn't belong. That I still took up space I didn't deserve.

A chill landed on my arms. I shivered when my hand moved of its own accord, adding a new item to the paper: *Stop seeing yourself as small.*

Whoa. That hadn't come from me.

"Okay, Agatha, was that you?"

I watched open-mouthed as my hand added new items to the list.

- Trust your instinct
- Do the things that make you feel strong
- Stop making lists

Well, Agatha had a sense of humor, anyway. I focused on one of the items she'd added. What made me feel strong?

I knew the answer, of course. In high school, I'd been a runner. I'd continued the hobby through college, adding weights after Gabe was born.

Working out made me feel strong. At my age, taking up running again would be difficult, but not impossible. I could start with a treadmill and weights and see what happened. Did Treater's Way have a gym?

Duh. *Magnolia* probably had a gym in the physical therapy clinic. I added visiting Lauren to my agenda for the week.

It still nagged at me that the ward Agatha had placed on me during college never wore off. That my own carelessness in life had created such a lasting impact. Who would I be if I'd returned twenty years ago like she'd expected me to?

I closed my eyes, thinking back to that period, and earlier, when my mother died. I'd felt this same restlessness then, this same call to act. I'd emptied that pain into a man. Ray Chase. Ethan's best friend until something happened, and they became enemies. When he left, I'd channeled this restlessness into Jeff.

I dropped my pen and stood. What would happen if I used all my energy and power to become the best damn version of myself I could be?

The thought of it sent my nervous system into overdrive. But this didn't feel like an onset of a panic attack. It wasn't just my soul that longed for more. My body wanted to move.

I laced up my tennis shoes and wiggled my body. I wouldn't run, not yet, but I could take a walk. I didn't need to wait for Lauren or the gym. I'd work up a sweat on my way to Books and Brew. Some time in Illusion Square would make me feel better.

I could find a book about witchcraft. Buy some herbs. Talk to the tree.

And clear my damn head.

I marched down the stairs and past the house. It was only then I remembered it was July and not spring. That doggone Magnolia magic. But I was too amped up to care, and before I knew it my brisk walk was a fast jog. Then a sprint.

I should have stayed home.

CHAPTER TWENTY-FOUR

Illusion Square was packed, and I was a sweaty mess. I stood amidst the smartly dressed housewives, looking like a drowned nutria. Sweat ran down my back like a waterfall. The gleaming surfaces at Books and Brew reflected my blotchy red face and haggard hair from every angle, as if I needed the reminder of how I looked.

And I ached. Every part of my body protested my rash decision. My shoulders were nothing more than a series of tight knots. My knees locked up with every step. My legs were wobbly noodles.

So much for a leisurely stroll and a refreshing afternoon at the stores. I was going to guzzle iced tea then slink back to the House for a bath and a nap.

I thanked the woman behind the counter and held the cool glass to my head. It wasn't Ana, but the aquamarine-eyed beauty had that same look. It rang of knowledge and left me unsteady. When I turned toward the door, Lauren caught my eye and waved from her table in the far corner.

Of course she looked like that. Her cute blond ponytail shone, her perfect makeup looked freshly applied, and she sported one of those luxury brand athletic dresses that accented every angle of her perfect body.

She beckoned me over with a genuine smile that reminded me we weren't in high school anymore. We were on a path to friendship. And I didn't have to knock another woman down just because she was pretty or put together. Just because the world was petty didn't mean I needed to be.

She wasn't alone at the table. A man sat across from her with his back to me. She said something to him as I approached, and though I couldn't see him, his broad shoulders tensed under the flow of his salt-and-pepper hair.

Hair I recognized. Hair that made my heart hammer all the way into my toes and my stomach churn like it was making spoiled ice cream.

Lauren reached across her table and patted his hand. It was friendly, not flirty, but an odd stab of jealousy burned my throat. I grabbed a stack of napkins, dabbing sweat off my neck and forehead, literally squeezing it out of my hair before it dripped to the floor.

"Simone! I'm so glad to see you outside the Magnolia. Did you have a good run?" She gestured toward the empty chair between her and her companion. "Join us!"

Her words were chipper, but there was a clear thread of nerves weaved into her tone.

"It was a good run, thanks. I'm kind of a mess. I'd planned a walk, but you know how plans go."

My mind was frantically trying to work up an excuse not to join them at the table. But anything I might have said died on my lips when her companion turned to face me.

He held a frozen smile so tight his lips trembled with it. His green eyes locked onto mine and held me captive. My mind, in a panic, begged me to flee. But the intensity of his gaze rooted me to the spot.

This was more than a stomach churn. This was more than a vague sensation of nausea or the desire to ruin shoes. My stomach flipped upside down, turned eight cartwheels in succession, and spun in dizzying circles.

I couldn't breathe.

I couldn't speak.

I no longer cared how I looked or who was with us.

The world around me fell away, transporting me back to the summer after high school and the boy who'd shattered my heart to pieces.

The boy who was now a man. With the brightest, clearest green eyes I'd ever seen.

Eyes that had haunted my dreams for years.

The eyes of my wolf.

Of course it was him. No one had ever or would ever have that pull on me.

"Simone? You remember Ray Chase?" Lauren was either smoother than silk or the queen of cluelessness. Had I thought she was nervous moments earlier? Either way, I was grateful she could normalize the space. "Really, neither of us minds that you're fresh off a workout. We've all been there. Have a seat!"

My brain went on autopilot, and my body betrayed me. I took the seat she'd extended, trying to ignore the way my thighs stuck to the metal chair. I'd have to peel myself off when I stood up. I might stay here until the Square emptied so no one had to witness that mayhem.

"How have you been?" Ray was talking to me. His full, wide lips were moving, and he was chatting casually.

As if we'd been nothing more than acquaintances who said goodbye at graduation.

As if I hadn't seen him in wolf form and longed to throw my arms around him.

As if he hadn't stolen a piece of me thirty years ago.

"I'm great!" Was that my voice? Was that me sounding chipper and squeaky and lying?

"Well, I've been okay." I took a sip of tea to steady myself. This was ridiculous. It had been thirty years. I wasn't a hormonal young adult lusting after the star quarterback, all moody and broken from his injury and needy and sexy and ...

"I've had a tumultuous few weeks. But before that, things were pretty smooth." I choked out a laugh to soften my throat at my blatant lie. "How have the last thirty years treated you? I trust you've recovered?"

A shadow darkened his eyes. Either because I'd brought up the injury that ruined his football career or the memory of the time we'd been together. I didn't care either way. I hadn't intended it to be such a loaded question.

Not really. Not when the questions I wanted to ask were far deeper and painful. But I couldn't say any of that out loud. Not with Lauren here or in a public setting.

We'd kept our relationship quiet, enjoying each other and hiding away from the world that, inevitably, was going to bring us back to reality. Lauren had been with Ethan, and they'd all been friends. I was on the outskirts.

Until the injury. Ethan failed to block a tackle, Ray was injured, and their friendship ruptured.

Ray, in his pain, had turned to me. I, in my pain over my mother's sudden death, had needed him. I'd kept my time with Ethan a secret, not that I needed to. We weren't dating.

All of that was thirty-years ago. Surely, he was over it?

I was.

I rubbed at my throat as Lauren tried to smooth the tension at the table. So now even thinking a lie affected my body? Dude.

"It still gives me trouble, believe it or not." Ray smiled across the table at Lauren in a way that totally didn't make me see red. "My physical therapist has been working with me since I came back. She's got great hands."

Lauren flinched on my behalf at the unfortunate wording. Ray's thick brows furrowed. Even with my eyes fixed on my iced tea, I caught the subtle shake of her head. Were they a thing? She'd said she preferred to be alone. Maybe she'd lied to protect my feelings.

"Ray owns Lone Wolf Sentries," Lauren said to break the silence. "He started it, what, fifteen years ago?"

"Closer to twenty," Ray said. "Almost as soon as I returned."

My blood chilled. It had to be a coincidence. Twenty years ago was around the time Agatha's ward was supposed to wear off. It was when *I* was supposed to come home.

My heart would not let me believe he came back for me. No matter how badly I wanted to.

"I envy both of you for your travels. I never left." Lauren propped her chin on her hands. "I mean, I went to New Orleans for college with Ethan—sorry, Ray—but as soon as we split up I was right back here. I wouldn't mind seeing more of the world."

There was something so likable about this version of Lauren that I couldn't help but smile with her. She meant it, and she was truly not saying anything in a way that indicated she was trying to dredge up the past. My gut believed her—that she had changed after high school, had realized what she'd been like, and had done some growing up. I wondered how much of that had to do with her split from Ethan.

But why had she apologized to Ray after mentioning Ethan? Were they still on the outs? I didn't remember much about the game that caused his injury. Ethan had missed a tackle, but that could happen to anyone. Was there something more to it?

"There's still time for travel and shenanigans," Ray told Lauren.

"Absolutely," I said. I wanted to be part of the conversation, to stop the never-ending stream of chatter my brain was throwing at me. "The world isn't going anywhere."

The rest of the conversation flowed by with a detached sense of three people catching up on thirty years of mayhem. I did get out of them that Ray had never married and Ethan was clearly a sore topic of conversation.

But little more. After fifteen minutes that felt like fifteen years, the combined adrenaline of my stupid decision to exercise and bumping into my ex wore off. Bone-tired and soul-weary, I peeled myself off the seat.

"Well, it was good to see you both, but I need to get prepared for the week." Ray rose with me, taking my hand in his. I wanted to yank it away; I wanted to shrink from the heat of his touch. Instead, I stayed perfectly still.

"It was so good to see you again, Simone. You look fantastic." Heat transferred from his hands to mine, burning me to my core. His thumb stroked my fingers, lingering in place when I pulled my hand away.

"You, too." I tore my gaze from his to smile at Lauren. "It's good to see both of you."

It took all that I had not to scurry out the door. I might have run home had my body chosen that moment to remind me I was pushing fifty.

My hips throbbed. My knees ached. Some weird, shooting pain ran the length of my foot, from big toe to thigh.

But dammit, I would not hobble home. Unshed tears threatened me, building pressure so intense I bit my lip to keep them at bay. I was not going to collapse in Illusion Square. I just couldn't.

Ray's eyes were on me. I didn't have to turn to know that. His stare was fire on the back of my neck.

I stopped at the Mighty Oak, lowering myself to the concrete bench protecting its trunk. I ran my fingers in the crisp, cool water surrounding it, fixing my eyes on the compass rose. The compass rose made of the same concrete as the bench, with dust like glitter that shimmered when light filtered through the oak's branches.

This was too much. Another case of moving forward only to be pushed back. Was nothing in my past what I thought it was? I tried to remain calm. To remind myself that I had a list back at the house, that I still had a plan, and that Ray being back in town did not change my plan.

He was still watching me. I had to leave. To gather the strength to stand up and go back to the Magnolia so I could recover without being seen.

The leaves of the Mighty Oak bristled. There was no wind, but a cold blast of air coated me. It caused ripples in the water, vibrations that seemed to affect the flecks of silver. As I watched, they gathered in the center, forming an arrow pointing north. Away from the entrance to Illusion Square. Toward the small path in the forest that led God knows where.

I was on my feet again. Each step was a thousand tiny hammers to my body. I ignored it, crossing Illusion Square in the direction of the arrow. I didn't know where I was going, but when magical specks of dust point you somewhere, you go.

That's just sound logic.

Before I knew it, Illusion Square faded into the distance, and I was on a path to nowhere in the narrow but dense forest at its border.

CHAPTER TWENTY-FIVE

Okay, so not a path to nowhere. The forest was maybe half a mile deep, leading to a narrow footbridge that crossed sparkling bayou water to a raised island.

An island I knew. The moment I was on the other side of the bridge, magic engulfed me. It wasn't tangible, or even visible, it was just the sensation of *other*. And it was as familiar as putting on my favorite pajamas.

"I remember you, Bridge Island. I remember every inch of you."

An island cannot vibrate with joy, like a small dog that pees when you come home at the end of a long day. But it may as well have, because saying those words out loud brought every single memory of this island back to me.

To my right was a lovely cottage-style house. It was the house where the goddess Iris lived. The woman I'd seen at Gino's Pizzeria when I had dinner with Lauren. We'd been friendly in high school. She had embraced her magic before she was a teenager, shedding her old self to become who she was meant. I could picture her before as clearly as her after.

Continuing forward, I reached the center of this small but bustling island where Bridge House stood proud. It clearly had a glow-up in the past thirty years. I'd always thought it majestic, but the way the house stood court now put its past power to shame. Just like Iris, someone had figured out how to help the house become its greatest form.

I had to guess it was the woman with the long, chestnut brown hair rocking on its patio. She had an air about her, as if she and the house were one. In a moment of absolute longing, I imagined how that must feel. I wanted that with the Magnolia.

Crowded next to her on the swing was the mischievous older woman I'd seen talking to the Mighty Oak. I returned their friendly wave, their names dancing in the swarm of new memories before coming forward. Ruth was the older woman, former proprietor of Bridge House. Misty was the new owner.

Misty was a mermaid. She and Dimitri, the troll of North Bridge, protected the island. How did I know that?

"The island is welcoming you home, Simone." Iris launched down the stairs and pulled me into a warm embrace. Hair darker than night weaved coils around a perfectly made-up face. Thick, reddened lips planted a kiss on my cheek. Rainbows trailed the ground around her. "I'm so thrilled you're back. One more piece to the Treater's Way puzzle falling into place."

She held me at arm's length, her fierce golden eyes meeting mine.

"Complete your tour of the island, hon. Then come back to Bridge House and we'll all have dinner and get reacquainted, yeah?"

I couldn't speak. I only nodded, the hint of a smile teasing my lips. Only moments earlier, my body and soul were aching and world-weary. Now, a vibrant new energy infused me. With a last squeeze of her hand, I continued my journey.

Bridge Island wasn't large. You could explore the whole of it in a day without bumping into the same person twice. It earned its name because of the two bridges at opposite ends of the island. South Bridge was the footbridge I'd crossed into Illusion Square.

North Bridge was this one-lane, rickety as hell, terrifying traffic bridge that led to New Orleans. No one in their right mind would drive on that piece of—

Whoa. I stopped short near the foot of North Bridge. When I left thirty years ago, it was a death trap. Now ...

North Bridge had also gone through a glow-up. A literal one. The thing glowed like a gilded runway to the mundane world beyond. Without moving further, I knew there was a ramshackle cabin at the base of the bridge. And a troll lived there.

I didn't want to interact with a troll at the moment. Nor did I need to. My instincts guided me to the left, through more forest. In the distance, the soft twangs of a guitar drifted through the trees. There was an old caretaker's house on the outskirts of the island, and I smiled at the wave of nostalgia that only familiar music can foster.

But I knew where I was going at this point, and as more of the island made itself known to me, I couldn't wait to get there.

I cleared the forest and found what I'd been looking for. Exactly as I remembered it.

It wasn't much to look at. A simple park bench on the west side of the island, with dark green slats and brass fittings bolted to a small base of concrete. I rounded the bench, sat, and exhaled.

The bench itself was simple. But it had one hell of a view.

My back was to Bridge House. I'd have to peer over my shoulder and crane my neck to glimpse North Bridge. In front of me was a short embankment leading down to the bayou. And ahead of me was miles and miles of water.

Possibility.

That's the exact word Ray used when we sat on this bench thirty years ago, and pledged eternity to one another.

"Look out there, Simone. There's so much possibility beyond Treater's Way."

He folded me in his arms. My most favorite place to escape. His broad shoulders and tall frame shielded me from the world. Hid me from pain. The slight tug at my scalp as he twirled a strand of my curls in one finger. The silk of his hair kissing my cheek.

"We can go anywhere we want, as long as we're together."

Even at eighteen, I'd heard the fear in his voice. I'd understood he was trying to convince himself, shrouded himself in the naivete of youth. But I'd suppressed the panic that quickened my pulse, attributing it to the line of kisses he planted at my temple.

Our affair began late senior year, when his parents forced him to see Agatha. I was helping in the office a few times a week, already eighteen and clinging to the last piece of my mother's legacy.

By graduation, we were madly in love. Our passionate, but secret, affair manifested in stolen kisses under North Bridge and secret trysts at Bridge House. At the time, no one lived there but Ruth. We existed in a world of our creation, foolishly believing the bubble wouldn't burst.

"There's no one but us, Simone. We're all the family we need."

The water rippled, drawing me away from that night. The fattest, longest alligator I'd ever seen slowed its ascent on shore. I was strangely unafraid and recognized him in an instant.

"Hey, Norbert," I said to the gator. "Long time no see."

"So good to see you're home, Simone." He winked his singular eye at me. Did all the magical creatures in this town have one of something that should be a pair? "Finally figured out how to break your own ward, huh?"

"I, uh, have I?" I stuttered over my words, a rush of terror cooling my veins. What ward? And how had I broken it?

Norbert stared at me for a long moment. I stared right back.

"Keep going," he said. "You're almost there." He flicked his tail, angled his body, and slid into the water with a speed I wouldn't have thought capable of such a large alligator.

Keep going. Back into the memories unfolding on the island. A night I thought I'd never forget with Ray. When he slept the next morning, I'd crept out to go for a run.

I was on a perfectly good island. I could have run the length of it and been happy.

But deep down, I knew I was already letting go. Maybe I hadn't believed, even then, Ray's promise. Or maybe it was because I'd already made a promise of my own.

I'd been accepted to Tulane. Agatha and I had our plan. I was going to college and would complete my clinicals in New Orleans. Get the experience of a mundane, then return and take over at the Magnolia.

Helping Ray and processing my mother's death helped me find my calling. He wanted freedom from responsibility. He wanted to take to the open road, or the open bayou, and see what the world brought him.

I had a different path.

So instead of running on the island, I'd crossed South Bridge and headed to the track where I knew my friend Ethan would be about to start his morning workout. He'd brought muffins, as if he knew I would be there.

One hour. One hour with a good friend who let me feel safe and strong and required nothing of me. One hour with someone else who had goals and ambition, and who wasn't afraid to express them.

We'd just finished our run. I was teasing him for losing again.

"Lauren and Ray showed up." No one was around me, Norbert long gone, but I said it out loud just to break the silent pain of the memory.

Lauren, with her arms crossed and a smirk I wanted to punch off her face, watched us break up. Ray screamed at me, claiming I was a liar and a cheat. He'd charged at Ethan, who wrestled him to the ground but wouldn't fight him.

Ray crossed North Bridge that day.

And my heart shattered, squashing down a relief I didn't want to feel. I'd cried for hours right here on this same park bench. In a fit of teen angst, I'd uttered words of pain aloud.

I'm done feeling things so deeply they can rip me up inside. I don't need family, and I don't deserve a good one.

My throat was so constricted I could scarcely breathe. My stomach sour and raw. My voice a siren's song to my soul. I'd dealt myself a devastating blow, not yet understanding the power of my decisions, or how much my voice truly mattered.

I'm done with this town and every single memory of it. It'll take a miracle to bring me back to Treater's Way.

As the memory unfolded, a series of angry sobs erupted from a compartment deep within my heart that I'd sealed up tight and locked shut with a magical ward. Every moment of my first eighteen years rushed forward, fitting into the places where I'd created stories of my past to keep moving toward the wrong future.

Every vivid detail I'd glossed over. Every tiny voice I'd squelched. Every errant thought I'd ignored.

Including the mysterious meeting with Agatha the day she died. The woman, calling herself Stella, who'd rushed into my failed therapy clinic in need of assistance, telling me she was dying and didn't know who to leave her estate to.

To soothe her, I'd reached into my metaphorical drawer of therapy tools and brought out the one I'd deemed most effective.

The same technique I'd used with Doug.

The miracle question.

CHAPTER TWENTY-SIX

It'll take a miracle to bring me back to Treater's Way.

By the time I found my way back to the Magnolia, the sun was setting. I greeted House, longing for a shower and a chance to collect my thoughts. Thankfully, no alarm shrilled a warning when I arrived. I didn't have it in me to face Ray again. In any form.

More than a shower, though, I wanted someone to help me process everything I'd learned. I'd told Lauren I forgave her before I knew what she was apologizing for. I didn't know if I could retroactively unaccept an apology. Not that it mattered. Even with her claims to have changed, a part of me didn't trust her completely.

The Twins were still in the "no" column. Lydia hated me, and I hadn't seen hide nor hair of Lyra or her division of the Magnolia. And while Brianne would almost definitely provide an ear, I didn't feel right tearing her away from her family on a Saturday evening.

I finished cleaning up, wrapped myself in the softest pajamas known to humankind, and decided that reality TV would be my companion for the evening.

I should have been more surprised to see Agatha rocking in the living room.

Her form was solid, the same blue Afghan draped across her lap. She smiled at me, and it was a smile I remembered.

"So, you figured out how to break the ward."

"Did you know?" I sat across from her, pretending it was totally normal to have a conversation with a now-corporeal spirit. "You could have saved us both a ton of pain and effort if so."

"I had no idea." Agatha chuckled softly, her voice muffled as if she were talking from miles under the water. "It happened so quickly. I didn't know anything was wrong for another ten years. I wasn't quite myself after your mother's death. Do you remember?"

"Like it was yesterday." My own tears surfaced. I hadn't thought about my mother clearly in thirty years. It was like mourning her loss anew. "I remember taking over her position."

"You were an expert manager. Trained by the best." Agatha wiped at a mystical tear. "You would have taken over, if I'd let you. Slipped right into the monumental space your mother left behind."

"I didn't want to stay, though, did I?"

"Oh, part of you wanted to." She chuckled again, and it was like a warm blanket tucking me in at night. I'd laughed with her often. "Ultimately, you had to choose your own path. And I was concerned that—"

"That if I stayed here, my path would have been chosen for me." I leaned back, sinking into the couch. "It's why I felt so pulled in different directions. I wanted so many things. To stay here and manage the Magnolia. To travel the world with Ray. To establish myself as a therapist."

"In the end, pain made the choice for us." Agatha shook her head and sighed. "That's so often the way it happens."

"You couldn't have known I was casting my own spells. I didn't know myself. I've controlled every life choice, even when I shouldn't. All the times I'd doubted my abilities and told myself I wasn't capable of doing a thing. All the words I'd used to stand in my own way acted against me."

I'd blamed the town. Then Ray. Then Jeff. Even my son.

In the end, the only one I had to blame was myself.

"How could one sentence, an oath made in a moment of rage, affect so much?"

I expected the question to be rhetorical, but Agatha leaned forward with an answer that surprised me.

"You have to know, dear one, I had no idea you were a word witch." She reached for me, unable to make contact. "If I had, things would have been different. You gave no indication as a child."

"Is it hereditary?" Now that I'd said it out loud, my mouth went dry. I'd wondered where my magical abilities came from. But part of me was afraid to learn the truth. "Was my mother a witch, too?"

"No, dear. You didn't get this from your mother." Agatha's smile was as enigmatic as it was sad, and I knew what that meant. The father I'd never met.

I knew better than to prod for more. I'd done that a dozen times growing up. When it came to my father, both Agatha and my mom had been vaults.

"So I broke the ward when you came to visit me." I pulled up my notes from the meeting, some of which I'd shared with Ethan a week earlier. "Patient refused to give full name, asked to go by Stella only and paid in cash." I scrolled further. "Had an immediate and positive response to the miracle question technique."

"An act of desperation from a dying woman." Agatha shrugged her shoulders. "What can I say, it worked didn't it?"

"Stella, huh? The woman I saw had striking red hair and impeccable dress."

"I hoped you'd sense my presence or break the glamor." Agatha chuckled again. "And I'm a sucker for *A Streetcar Named Desire*."

"I'd said it would take a miracle to get me to return to Treater's Way." I wanted a cool drink of water, asked House for it, and took my time drinking it down. "What did I say to you that worked?"

"At the end of our session, as you walked me to the door"—she sighed, as if suddenly exhausted—"you said we'd made a miracle happen. It only proved I was right."

Agatha's form faded in, out, and back in. I was running out of time with her. I didn't understand why I'd said we both had a miracle. It wasn't my usual choice of words. Maybe part of me had known it was her.

Or maybe I was just ready to come home. Agatha wouldn't have the answer to that, though. And I still had questions.

"It proved you were right about what, Agatha?"

"About you, Simone Cecelia Bardot, who was clever enough to keep her own name when she married. You fought against the ward, even without realizing it. Even when you thought you didn't deserve it." She tapped the edge of her rocker. "You were meant to be here, CC. Never forget that. I believe in you."

Her encouragement filled the air like a distant tune. I leaned forward to catch it.

"Are you leaving, Agatha?"

"Not quite, dear. I'm here until the next board meeting, no matter what." She'd never sounded more tired. "Now listen closely, it took a lot of energy for House to bring me to you, and we're running out of time."

"You can stay a moment longer." The words flowed from me like a cool breeze. "I will hold you here, Agatha."

"Well done, dear." Her form solidified. Her shoulders dropped in relaxation. Power traveled between us, streams of light in varying shades of blue.

"Tell me all that you can, Agatha."

She heaved a breath and closed her eyes.

"Mind the Twins. They are mostly harmless but can be mischievous. They will test you as often as you let them, but they won't stand in your way as long as you push back. Sweet Lauren has grown a lot over the years. You'll have obstacles to overcome, but she's solid as they come. Relish your friendship with Brianne. I believe you two are soul mates, such as friends go. It's why she's here."

I'd had that feeling about Brianne from the moment we met. She and I were meant to do great things together. With each word, hope glimmered stronger inside me. I had everything I needed now to repair the damage.

"If you make things right with Doug, your other patients will fall in line. There's nothing wrong with your methods, Simone." Her voice hardened. "But not everyone wants to know an end is in sight."

She was fading again. Fatigue hammered at my limbs. Sweat coated my upper lip. Holding her here was taking a toll on both of us.

"One last thing." There was a warning in her tone that set my teeth on edge. "The chains of magic can bind, but the bonds of family can shatter even the strongest link."

"What?" As far as warnings went, it was a doozy. A shiver shot up my spine, like lightning in a summer storm. "What does that mean, Agatha?"

Her lips were moving, but I couldn't make out words. House seemed to shudder with the efforts to hold her in place. I was sweaty and exhausted.

"I love you, Sweets." With her final words drifting through the air, Agatha disappeared. The blue blanket flitted to the ground. The rocker swayed a moment longer, moving with the momentum of her presence. Then it too stilled, and I was alone.

CHAPTER TWENTY-SEVEN

There was a first for everything. And this was definitely the first time I'd visited a patient's house.

I hoped it would be the last.

As I approached the small but charming blue home set back from town square in a little cul-de-sac, I couldn't help but wonder if this was a terrible mistake.

It probably was.

But it was the only mistake I knew how to make at the moment. I hummed Lizzo on the sidewalk, trying to pump myself up. It worked. Sort of.

The door opened before I reached it, and Doug glowered from the doorway. It was just after lunchtime on a Sunday afternoon, before the time I suspected old men took naps but after the time that I would interrupt food. I was assuming Doug's life was regimented, of course, and given he was wearing the same slacks from our first session—with a pressed polo in favor of the button up—my assumption appeared accurate.

"I'm not coming back, and it's damn inappropriate you're on my doorstep."

"It sure is." I held up my hands in surrender. "I've never done it before, Doug. But I had something important to tell you, and I kind of hoped I could talk you into hearing me out."

Doug crossed his arms, a physical gesture that reflected his well-guarded shield. He dipped his eyebrows low. Whatever I said, he was going to be reading my every emotion. I swallowed, making sure my throat was clear.

"I have a story I'd love to tell you, Doug. Do you mind listening to it? I promise it won't take up much more of your afternoon." I took a cautious step forward. "After you hear it, I'll leave. You don't have to promise to come back. But I'll hold your space for another two weeks. Just in case."

Football blared in the background noise from his open door. Birds chirped from the trees surrounding his house. A car revved its engine. Doug stared at me, unmoving.

"You know, Doug, I recently discovered that as a word witch I have the power to compel people to do things they may not want to." I paused a beat. "Even myself, as it turns out. I've had this *ability* my entire life and didn't know it. I even used it without meaning to."

I paused to let him read me, holding his gaze. His arms dropped slowly to his side. "Say what you gotta from there."

Okay. It was progress.

"It's pretty scary, actually. This new power that isn't new at all. I'm tempted to ignore it. After all, learning to use it properly sounds super hard. Even though I've been in a lot of pain lately—and I mean a lot of pain, Doug—the pain I know now is still more comfortable than the pain of going through to the other side. Know what I mean?"

He might have nodded. It was such a slight dip of his chin it could have been anything. But he wasn't telling me to shut up or slamming the door in my face, so I would take it.

"Or I could harness it, and do the right thing with it. Help people relax a bit during sessions. That way, they can allow themselves to see past their anxiety or anger to the core of their pain."

I took another step forward.

"That's a pretty powerful tool in therapy, you know? I can get past the armor people place around their thoughts and feelings, the barrier that trauma forces us to create, so they can clear it. And live the life they are meant to live."

Another step. Doug stiffened, but aside from the twitch of his lips, he didn't move.

"But I would never, ever, ever force people to do something they didn't want to do. I wouldn't rush them to heal or put them under hypnosis or anything like that. Not on purpose, Doug."

Crickets. Okay, Simone, just keep going.

"Did you hear the rumors about my husband? Did you know I'd caught him cheating a week before Agatha passed?"

He still wasn't speaking, but his eyebrows lifted a fraction of an inch.

"You didn't. That's a relief, I'll be honest with you. Because only a few people from this town could know that, and I don't want to believe they are the gossip spreading type. Probably the only thing people knew until the other day was that Agatha left her practice to an outsider. Or someone that used to be a local, because I was born and raised here after all, but chose to leave and not come back like a damn fool."

Doug snorted in laughter, and I breathed relief when his shoulders sagged. He was hearing me and reading my point.

"Ah, that was the rumor spread about me. The truth is more complicated than that. It usually is, right? For example, your truth is that you promised your wife you'd go to therapy after she died."

I paused again. Light tears shimmered in his eyes.

"That's only part of the truth though, right? The full truth is that every week you show up to therapy for someone to talk to. And it reminds you of the immense pain you must have felt when she died. Pain you can't let go of, because letting go of it would mean letting go of your wife's memory."

I'd made it to the door and kept my voice low in case someone nearby had super hearing. Tears streamed freely down Doug's lined face.

"When you came to your first session, I was trying so hard to be a good textbook therapist that I forgot to be a good personal therapist. I know that sounds weird, but the truth is that I'm at my best when I channel my emotions. I've never been good at keeping people at a distance, even my patients. I like to let them know they aren't alone in their struggles. And that their therapist is imperfect, too."

I risked reaching for Doug's hand and was grateful he allowed me to take it. I cupped his hands in mine.

"I understand your pain, Doug. It's not the same as mine, but I get it. And I understand the pressure you must have felt as a police officer to toe a specific line because I'm feeling pressured to be the kind of therapist Agatha was."

I let his hand drop.

"But we're different. We're not human. And we're not supernatural. We're both, and we have abilities that alter the way we do our jobs. The way we feel love. Even the way we interact with strangers." I swiped at my face, and the wet I felt cooling my cheeks.

I shrugged my shoulders up to my ears, then let them drop all the way down.

"It was never my intention to cast a spell on you, Doug Holloway. If I created emotions in you with my words, I'm well and truly horrified about that. And I'm incredibly sorry." I swallowed, checking my throat. All clear. "Please use *your* ability to see how sincere I am."

Doug cleared his throat, and I waited in case he was prepared to speak. When he said nothing, I rushed out the rest of my message.

"I'd like to help you find a way to manage your pain, Doug, without letting go of the parts of it that are you. I think your wife would like that. And I think you would, too. If that's something you want to try, even if it means moving through a new, scary kind of pain, then I'll see you tomorrow morning. But you should know, everything is going to look different."

I waved and trotted down the stairs without waiting for a reply. I'd done what I could. Doug would have to take the next step.

Besides, I still had a lot of work to do. And my last sentence surprised even me. I rushed home, eager to see what my new therapy office was going to look like.

CHAPTER TWENTY-EIGHT

Ethan was leaning against the front gate when I returned to the Magnolia. I clamped down on my disappointment. So much for seeing the new digs. I didn't fully mind, though. Ethan was on my list. Plus, the man was easy on the eyes.

He wore a wrinkled concert t-shirt over jeans that hugged his hips just right. Worn sneakers covered feet crossed at the ankles. And a grin I could only describe as sheepish covered his face.

"Well, well, if it isn't the pack leader of Louisiana justice." I pushed his shoulder playfully. "You could have told me you were a wolf shifter when we first talked, you know."

"I couldn't be sure you would accept it." He looped his arm in mine and followed me around back. "We never talked about magic back in high school."

"That's true. Seems like we all had secrets." I gestured for him to come upstairs. The scent of fresh muffins wafted toward us when the door opened. "Looks like House knew you were coming."

"Best house ever." He patted the wall like it was an obedient puppy. "House is looking better. Fresh coat of paint. New windowpanes. Pretty sign."

House preened in its own way, adding a sparkle to the chrome fixtures in the breakfast area as Ethan sat.

"House feels better about itself. Did you see the new garden boxes in the backyard? I hope I'm not expected to tend to them. My thumb could not be more brown."

Ethan strolled to look out the window while I piled two muffins on plates and poured coffee.

"Those are lovely." Ethan nodded his thanks and took the seat across from me. "I could get used to this."

"Just like old times." I took a huge bite and laughed to myself. "Well, not exactly."

"I'm sorry I didn't tell you. About my supernatural side." He picked at a crumb. "I wanted to, especially in high school. Always pissed me off that you ran faster when I'm a wolf and you're a human."

"Except I wasn't, was I? And I always told you I was faster. So it happened." I pointed at my chest. "Word witch, dude. What I say happens."

"Huh." Ethan stared into his coffee. "Well, that makes me even madder."

We finished the muffins over lighthearted banter, enjoying the small bit of peace between us. This was the version of Ethan I remembered, the one I could joke with and be myself around. I'd forgotten him, too, when I'd cursed myself. The memory of our times working out together being little more than a distant memory.

"Want more coffee?" I stood to refill my cup, steeling myself for the hard questions I wanted to ask while I had him.

"Another cup and I'll be awake all night." Ethan bumped my shoulder on his way to the sink.

When we were back at the table, Ethan sat back and steepled his fingers, lifting one eyebrow.

"I take it Lauren updated you?"

His rich complexion seemed to deepen. I was going to have to be careful what I said to Lauren. I knew they were close, but it seemed like they shared things with one another freely.

"I got all my memories back yesterday." I had to admit, I enjoyed the pure shock that crossed over his face. Take that, Lauren. "After I left her and Ray at the Square, I crossed South Bridge. I figured out why I lost them in the first place."

I filled him in on my trip to the bench and how I discovered I'd warded myself away.

"I remember everything about my last day in Treater's Way now." A fresh tremor shook my lip. "Even if I don't want to."

Ethan's eyes dropped to his lap.

"I always hated the way we said goodbye, Simone."

"Except we didn't say goodbye, did we?" I tapped on the table to get his attention. "You were fighting with Ray when I fled. What's the piece of the story that I'm missing, Ethan?"

He fiddled with the hem of his shirt. Bless him, I wanted to iron it.

"Well, I guess it's okay to tell you. Now that you know more about our ..." His voice trailed, and he turned his hand in a *fill-in-the-blanks* gesture.

"Heritage?" I supplied.

"Sure, let's call it that." He said with a chuckle. "Ray's family and my family are from rival wolf packs. Both moved here to escape the pack mentality. Wolf life can be volatile, and neither of our family's wanted any part of that."

"Were they friends?"

"No. They weren't mortal enemies, but there was enough tension to keep them from getting along. Ray and I developed a friendship despite that. Our families tolerated each other because he and I were close. I've never had a friend that tight." For a moment, his voice cracked, and I felt his sadness as if it were my own. "Well, except Lauren."

"But it's different with a witch, right?" He drew in his eyebrows at my query. "I mean, isn't there a wolf bond or something that creates a connection?"

"With a romantic mate, yes. Once a wolf meets their fated mate, there's nothing like it." Ethan's eyes lifted to the ceiling, then he shook his head to clear whatever thought invaded that he didn't want to share. "So I'm told."

For whatever reason, he'd made himself nervous. I gestured for him to continue without probing, even though my curiosity was begging me to ask more questions.

"Ray and I were close because we both understood what it meant. To be a shifter. To escape from family responsibility." He swallowed his own pain down to continue. Poor Ethan, he really had lost a good friend.

"When Ray turned seventeen, he started to change. He'd always been fierce and intense, but there was a new edge to him. It was ... gosh, what's the word?"

"He was feral," I said. I remembered feral Ray. That hint of wild just at the edges of his emotions. Always on the border between losing control and reigning himself in. It was terrifying and intoxicating.

Ethan read it on my face and offered a nod of solidarity.

"He was. When his grandfather came to visit over Thanksgiving, he explained that Ray was the new alpha. The old one had been killed in some stupid battle. Ray was expected to take over immediately, control his feral side, and become a proper pack leader. Ray could see his future in the NFL disappearing. He begged to at least finish high school. His family backed his decision."

"But his grandfather didn't?"

"His grandfather didn't have a choice. Ray was the alpha. Just learning he was meant to take over gave him a strength no one could match." Ethan gazed out the window, getting lost a moment before continuing. "Some of this story is his to tell. He was angry after that. All the time. Too strong and too out of control."

Ethan rose and paced the small space, just as he'd done at one of our first meetings.

"Ray was fighting every instinct he had. It kept him on edge. Affected every relationship he'd developed. Once we found out the battle that made him alpha had been with my family's pack, we weren't the same. I swear, he took the piss out of me for any small perceived infraction.

"Then one bad game, we miscommunicated a play. I veered left while he went right." Ethan dropped into his chair. "You know the rest."

"An injury that ended his career before it began. He lost his scholarship. The future he'd planned for and dreamt about." I didn't need Ethan to tell me that part. His loss and my loss were what bound us. "He blamed you."

I'd spent every waking moment with Ray after the injury, keeping my friendship with Ethan quiet only for the sake of his anger as he railed against the best friend who had betrayed him. I didn't have the details. Until now.

"To this day, he insists I did it on purpose." He dug his fingers into his hair. "But I didn't. I swear it, Simone."

Ray had never told me that he was a wolf. As close as I thought we'd been, the truth was we'd kept a lot from each other. The same held for Ethan. We'd kept our discussions about fitness and college. All the while, he harbored this pain.

I pulled my chair closer and put an arm over his hunched shoulders.

The man sitting next to me was very different from the one I'd known back then. It only made sense. We all had thirty years to mature and make grown-up mistakes.

Had Ray matured as well? I believed so. I thought back to the many times I'd caught Ray in his wolf form, watching me from afar, sorrow in his eyes. The way he'd protected me when Jeff appeared. He'd shown a restraint I'd never seen from him when we dated.

"I believe you, Ethan. And one day, he will too."

My throat was crystal clear. I knew it was true. If we were all back here in our tiny hamlet of a town, we'd have to find ways to get along. I'd bump into Ray again. Surely Ethan and Ray's paths crossed.

He angled his face closer to mine. Red rimmed his eyes. They drifted to my lips.

The air between us sizzled with an electricity that cut to my core. Desire yawned and stretched like a cat inside me, awake after a long hibernation. It looked at the hotness that was Ethan and nodded. Yes, please.

Whoa.

I shot to my feet. It was my turn to pace.

Nine days. It had only been nine days since I found out about the Magnolia. Add a week to that since I walked in on my husband mid-coitus. Then Ray resurfaced, along with all my memories.

Oh yeah, and I was a witch who was using her powers without knowing it.

It was a lot.

Ethan was rubbing the back of his neck like it burned. He couldn't stop fidgeting in his seat. He was embarrassed and adorable and nervous and hot as hell.

But the last thing I needed was a romantic entanglement. And no matter how much the thought of, ahem, physical relief appealed to me, the truth was I didn't want any romance in my life. Maybe Lauren had it right. Being alone sounded really nice right now.

I had too much to figure out. I wanted to repair my relationship with my son. I was about to take over a major business. I had a list, dammit, and boning wasn't on it.

I wanted to stand on my own two feet. To make decisions based on me, the Magnolia, and no one else.

Hot, sweaty sex was going to have to wait. How to let him down gently?

"I'm going to need a divorce lawyer, Ethan. A fierce one." It was an awkward way to express it, but it worked. Ethan put on his game face.

"Go on."

"Jeff will claim I hexed him. I don't know if a court would believe him or not. I don't want to run the risk of him making a play for the Magnolia."

"Most divorces don't wind up in court, Simone." Ethan twisted his lips into a smirk. "Did you? Hex your ex?"

"Um, yeah." I pulled my chair back to the table and sat opposite him. The space helped steady my pulse. "It was kind of an accident, and I think I fixed it already." I sighed. "I should probably go back to New Orleans and check."

"Will he fight a divorce?" Ethan asked.

I took a moment to mull it over, listening to what my instincts said on the matter.

"Maybe a week ago. But now?" I shook my head. "I'm pretty sure he's as done with me as I am with him."

"Let me know when you plan to return, and I will draw up the papers and have them served before you get there." He pulled out his phone and made a note before returning it to his pocket. "As far as the Magnolia, you're covered. I'm a damn good attorney."

At his sly smile, desire perked up again. Down, girl.

"Thanks, Ethan. You're a good friend."

"I'm glad I could help." He rose, pulling me into an embrace that was, somewhat disappointedly, friendly. "And I'm glad you're home."

"Me, too." I walked him to the door. "See you soon?"

"I'll have my office call you." With a kiss on my cheek that lingered slightly longer than a peck, he stepped out. "In three weeks, everything will be settled, Simone. You'll see."

Three weeks. It felt like an eternity.

CHAPTER TWENTY-NINE

I spent the remainder of Sunday writing a note to Gabe. It was too much for a text, and he didn't answer my phone calls. Probably because he thought it was a stranger who kept calling the wrong number.

I needed to make headway with him. I was terrified our relationship was permanently damaged. And I had no idea what Jeff was saying to him about the mother he'd forgotten. Did he have a sense of loss? Or was he thriving without the weight of a difficult mother holding him down?

I wrote myself raw in the note. There were things I wanted to say in person, and if I rambled about magic and discovering I was a witch, I'd just sound like a crazy woman. But I reiterated how proud I was of the young man he'd become and how our problems were a result of my own issues and nothing he'd ever done. I must have used the words *I'm sorry* a dozen times over two pages, but I didn't care.

I couldn't repair things overnight. But I needed to clear the infectious parts of our wounded relationship to give us a chance to heal. I folded the paper and tucked it into an envelope, writing his name in red, his favorite color.

Holding the letter in front of my face, I closed my eyes and channeled all my energy into my throat. It hummed, the vibration coming from the floorboards beneath me. When I finally spoke, my voice had a different timbre. It was deeper and richer. I liked it.

"This letter will find its way to my son Gabe. When he touches it, the hex I placed on him nine days ago will break. He will remember I exist and read it with an open heart." There was more I wanted to say. I wanted to command him to forgive me. To reach out immediately.

But I couldn't do that to him. I needed to be more conscious about the way I used my power. I couldn't manipulate or force anyone. I didn't mind undoing my curse, but I couldn't undo the past no matter how much I wanted to.

"The rest will be up to Gabe."

I opened my eyes when the letter disappeared.

That night I crawled into bed focused on my therapy clinic downstairs. I'd changed the waiting area on my first day, but throughout the week the main office held the same tired, boring look it had when I first arrived.

I had to hope that Doug would keep his appointment, and I'd promised him things would be different. I wanted to keep that promise.

It was time for me to be different, too.

I loved my second-natured empathy. It was a gift that I read other people's emotions and carried them with my own. A gift I could and should use to be the most effective therapist possible.

But for too long, I'd swung between hyper-emotional self-sabotage and callous disregard for others. It was time to strike the right balance. To know myself well enough that I could trust my choices.

And to use that confidence, and my natural gifts, to help others. The way I'd wanted to back when I was fresh out of high school and eager about my future.

I'd done everything I could to rectify my mistakes. It was time to let things play out.

As I drifted to sleep, for the first time in longer than I could recall, I felt good about myself. Empowered and strong.

And just like that, I could see the therapy room. I drifted off to sleep, a smile teasing my lips.

I couldn't wait to go to work in the morning.

CHAPTER THIRTY

I squealed as I surveyed the office, jumping up and down and clapping my hands like a little girl who discovered a magic machine that spits out pancakes.

It. Was. Perfection.

Gone was the dark wood and stuffy furniture. Gone was the tell-me-about-your-mother couch. Gone was the heavy desk barricading me from my clients.

A massive window on the far wall reflected a tranquil basin that surrounded Bridge Island. Birds took flight and water bugs danced along the surface of the water. Norbert the gator cut through the sheen, cast one eye in my direction, then continued past. Moss dripped from trees, their knobby knees poking up around their trunks.

It was the view from my park bench.

Several large, potted plants with leafy evergreens surrounded the base of the window. Long, beige curtains framed the view. There were several lamps of brushed gold with drum-shaped lamp shades in a simple white.

In the center of the room, atop a lovely throw rug that swirled tan, cream, and sage, were two chairs opposite a matching couch. All three were invitingly soft, with thick cushions and simple legs of light wood. The arrangement gave me options, and I didn't need a desk in here when I had a perfect one upstairs.

The wall on the left contained a large bookshelf in the same wood as the chairs. The bottoms of the shelves were filing cabinets. I didn't need to check them to know they would only open to my touch. On the shelves were a few decorative items and multiple copies of some of the books I used to recommend to clients.

And it only got more perfect from there. The corner by the door housed a water feature, a tinkling fountain lit in gold hues. It would soothe clients and ensure privacy if someone was in the waiting room.

My diplomas and certifications were hung in simple gold frames that matched the lamps. An oil painting covered the space over the couch. It was stunning. I peered close to take it in.

The Magnolia. In perfect detail, including the sign I'd created. Someone had put a lot of work into this. There was an art store in Illusion Square, could someone there have created this? In the corner was a small signature. D-RAP. I squealed again. He was a New Orleans native whose work I recognized.

"What's with all the squealing in here?" Brianne took two steps in, turned in her own circle, and joined the squeals. "Simone, this is perfect!"

"Right?! Everything is going to be perfect. Or as perfect as things can get." I grabbed her close and squeezed her tight.

"Well, this is a new version of you. Honey, I can't breathe." I released her, but she laughed and hugged me close again. "A lot's happened since Friday, huh?"

"Ugh, you have no idea. I wish I had time to give you a recap. But I don't, so shoo." I pushed away with a grin, fixing my hair. "My first client will be here any minute, and I want everything to look professional." Her brow furrowed, a fraction of an inch. I squeezed her hand. "He'll be here, Brianne. I just know it."

And there it was in my voice again, that rich timbre. Like I weaved words out of silk.

Sure enough, we walked into the waiting room, and Doug sat at one of the chairs, thumbing through a magazine. Gumbo snoozed on his lap. So much for professional.

"Good morning, Doug." I pasted a welcoming smile on my face, even though my insides were twisted into a thousand excited, nervous knots. Not like he couldn't tell. "Would you like to come in?"

Gumbo hopped off his lap, returning to the chair he vacated as soon as he stood. I extended my arm, gesturing for Doug to go in first. I wanted to catch every minute of his first impression.

He didn't clap. Or squeal. Not that I expected him to. He took a slow circle with the most impassive face ever. I stood by the door, my hands clasped behind my back. My thumbs twiddled a thousand circles while I waited for a response.

Just when I thought I couldn't take the suspense anymore, Doug crossed his arms and nodded.

"Looks good," he said. He pressed his lips together and nodded again. "Looks real good, Simone."

"I'm glad you like it." The calmness in my voice was remarkable. "Would you like to take a seat?"

Doug studied me a moment longer. Then, with a grin the devil would envy, he sat in one of the chairs. I couldn't help the laugh that escaped. I grabbed my notebook and plopped down onto the couch.

We spent several minutes gazing out the window, watching clouds float by. The tip of a vivid fin dipped out of the water, too large to be an everyday fish.

"What would you like to discuss today, Doug?"

"Saw the flower beds out front. They need tending."

"Yes, they do." I stifled a chuckle. "We have some overgrowth happening in the back, too. House and I are working on it."

"I can help," he replied. "Been mowin' the lawn for years, may as well do some gardening while I'm at it."

Huh. So that solved the mystery of the lawn. I guess the house didn't do everything with magic, which was good to know but also disappointing. I hated dishes.

"I'd sure appreciate it, Doug. Yard work is not one of my strengths."

"What are your strengths, Simone?"

I took a moment to assess his tone. Doug knew every emotion I was cycling through. Even the ones I was trying to hide. But he was the blankest of slates, and I hadn't known him long enough to read his tell. If he had one.

I wasn't sure if he was teasing me or challenging me. So I decided to answer honestly.

"Well, owning up to my mistakes is a pretty big strength. Not everyone can do that. I'm a damn good listener." I crossed my legs and smiled. "And I know when someone's avoiding their own crap by focusing on someone else's."

He drew in a sharp breath that made me hold mine. Then, the most amazing thing happened.

Doug Holloway laughed.

He had one of those full-body laughs that fills a room. The kind you can't help but laugh along with. He slapped his knee and clapped his hands. When he finally stopped, wiping tears from his eyes, I realized the room hadn't been perfect before.

The design was perfect. But the room needed this. Someone laughing in a way they didn't intend to. Someone letting themselves be vulnerable. Someone connecting with their therapist in a way that allows them to feel safe enough to relax.

That is the space where growth begins. Even on a couch.

"So Doug," I said once he was still. "What would you like to talk about today?"

Doug stared at his lap a moment longer, inspecting fingernails cut to the skin. When he looked at me, all mirth was gone. In its place was a soft, raw sadness I understood completely.

"Well, Simone"—he drew in a shuddery breath—"I think I'd like to tell you about my wife."

"I think I'd like that too." I positioned my pen over my pad, ready to take notes on my first real session with Doug Holloway.

CHAPTER THIRTY-ONE

By Friday of that week, Brianne, Lauren, and I had taken to eating lunch at the breakroom table. It was a mostly comfortable silence. At my request, Brianne had the phone forwarded to voicemail. It rang on occasion, a single sound followed by a beep. Each time, Bri twitched.

"You can relax for an hour and enjoy your lunch, Brianne." I pushed the lettuce on my plate around, nudging it aside to eat the few remaining chunks of cheese. As far as I was concerned, once you cleared all the good stuff out of a salad, it wasn't worth eating anymore.

"She's right," Lauren said. Lauren ate her lettuce, which was a much darker green than mine. Probably healthier. But blech. "I like this new policy, Simone."

"I'm not in a position to make policies yet, but this is a good start." I wanted to accept the compliment at face value, but I couldn't. And my so-called policy had really been more of a suggestion we'd all embraced.

Since Doug had given me a second chance, not a single client had canceled. My calendar was full again. There were mixed reactions to the new office, as well as my methods, but most of my clients were remaining open-minded.

I was making progress. They were making progress, too. It felt great. But it was exhausting. I no longer had the stamina of a naive young therapist treating human patients.

I had yet to dip my toes fully into the business-end of running the

Magnolia. But one thing had become very obvious very quickly: the place was full of workaholics. Brianne spent a distracted 15-minutes at her desk, balancing a fork in one hand and the phone in the other. Both the medspa and the salon were booked solid. Lauren barely poked her head out between sessions.

The few times I'd run into her in the breakroom, her stomach growled so loudly we couldn't carry on a conversation. That wasn't necessarily a bad thing given we were still on uneven footing. We'd yet to discuss our awkward encounter in Illusion Square or her relationship with Ray.

Even I knew the executives weren't creating a sustainable business practice. How could we claim to be a wellness center if the people who ran it were perpetually underfed and overstimulated? Even if every division had assistance, there was no way we were operating at full potential. Not when the folks at the top barely gave themselves time to eat.

So, I'd suggested we all take one hour of our day away from our respective desks or clients to eat lunch and commune.

Almost everyone was on board with the idea.

"One day, the Twins will join us." Brianne nabbed a french fry from the shared basket in the center of the table. Salads were great and all, but everyone needed a few french fries to perk up their day.

As if she'd heard Brianne, the massive door to the medspa opened. Lydia sauntered out with a client I recognized as one of my own. Cindrette offered me a friendly wave before hugging Lydia goodbye.

Lydia paused for a moment, one hand on the door to the medspa. Her eyes briefly met mine and held. I braced myself for either her wave of anger or the charm spell she liked to put on me. Neither came. Her lip twisted on one side, like an almost smile. She might have nodded her head hello. Then she disappeared inside.

I took it as progress.

"The Twins will join us for lunch one day. When they're ready," I said. I closed my eyes for a moment, to give myself time to assess whether I was casting a spell or speaking my hopes out loud.

As it turned out, there was a difference. I was learning to distinguish between my normal voice and my magic voice. It took more than hearing the change in pitch. I had to pay attention to my emotions, too, something I'd apparently stopped doing for far too long.

Given that most of my days I was still in turmoil, it was harder than it should have been. But the more I practiced, the better I got. And if constantly analyzing what I was thinking or feeling kept me from accidentally hexing someone, then I was all for it.

Happily, my throat was clear and my stomach calm. I believed the Twins would come around if I gave them time. I didn't want or need to manipulate them.

Or anyone else.

"They'll feel better after the board meeting." Lauren dragged a fry across the leftover ranch dressing from her salad before popping it into her mouth. I couldn't explain why, but it made me like her better. "Can you believe it's only two weeks from today?"

Not only was I improving at reading my own emotions. I was getting better at paying attention to others', too, which was how I knew that Lauren was nervous. There was the slight flicker of her fingers, as if she were trying to keep them from trembling. Her voice was high and tight. And her toe tapped a consistent, but discordant, tune under the table.

It was nice to finally feel like I was out of survival mode. To be able to breathe in and take stock of the people around me. It was even nicer to have the power not only to recognize their needs, but to meet them.

When I first arrived at the Magnolia, I'd thought the lobby was empty. I'd worried the business was failing, when what had actually failed was my ability to see things for what they were. Even during our quiet lunch hour, a stream of supernatural creatures moved through the lobby. A minotaur hobbled through the door to physical therapy. A human-passing warlock bid us hello on his way to the salon.

My new position, so far, was exhilarating. There was no way I was going back to New Orleans. I barely remembered the Simone who'd stood outside the Magnolia a mere two weeks prior, picturing herself as the main character in a movie, before her life was changed forever.

But I'd yet to share my intentions with anyone other than Ethan. Maybe I was afraid that if I told them I was staying and screwed up again I'd make an even bigger mess. Or maybe it was because I wanted everyone to accept me for who I was before I made declared myself Supreme.

Besides, Agatha's final warning still lived in my head rent free.

The chains of magic can bind, but the bonds of family can shatter even the strongest link.

What the heck did that even mean?

Whatever it was, I got the feeling the board meeting was the first of my hurdles, not the last. And friendship was a two-way street. If Lauren was nervous, the least I could do was soothe her. I closed my eyes again and searched for my gift. It was cool in my throat, like I'd swallowed concentrated peppermint.

When I opened my eyes and spoke, it was as if my words were carried on the wind. I couldn't hear my own voice, but I felt the power of it all the way down to my root.

"No one in the Magnolia can see or hear us for the next five minutes. Not even our mystical protector."

I hadn't actually known Gumbo was near until I noticed Brianne's hand was under the table. He let out an indignant meow and scampered away from the table. Brianne wiped her fingers on a napkin and grinned at me.

"I know they're bad for him, but he's so dang cute."

"He is. But this is for the three of us only." I wasn't sure exactly what I was going to say, but I had their attention. "Agatha and I had a nice chat last Sunday. And an unexpected visit to Bridge Island helped me recover my memories from my youth. All my memories."

I halted to stare pointedly at Lauren, whose pretty peach skin blushed red.

"I'm settling into my position as the Division Head for Magnolia Mental Health. I wanted you both to know I have every intention of accepting my position at the next board meeting."

The response was more than I'd expected. Brianne leaned all the way over to hug me. Lauren bounced up and down, clapping in a way that reminded me of her old cheerleader days. Without the self-important smirk. They started speaking over each other, peppering me with questions.

I appreciated their enthusiasm, but apparently, I wasn't done speaking. I held up a hand to silence them. Vivid blue lightning danced across my palm. Whoa.

"But my position as Supreme is not secure. Someone is coming."

Bolts flew from my fingers, zapping the air around us. They barraged the table with a dozen charred scratches.

"Who is coming, Simone?" Lauren ran her hands over her arms with a shudder.

"I'm not sure," I answered between chattering teeth. I had a chill of my own. "All I know is they're coming to challenge me, and I'll need all the support I can get."

It felt like my body was acting without my control. I had no idea what I would do next. I placed both hands on the table, rubbing them like I was trying to start a fire. My palms were like ice against the charred surface. I exhaled, and the marks of my lightning attack disappeared.

Well, that was cool.

"What I need to know today is whether or not I have your support."

"Brianne?" I turned to her first, already knowing the answer. She laid her hand over my left hand, still resting on the table.

"Abso-effing-lutely." I'd take it. It was as close to a cuss word as Brianne would get.

"Lauren?" Even with this power weaving through me, my uncertainty was apparent in my voice. I did my best to hold still and keep her stare.

I had to admit, her confident smile and the fact that she didn't hesitate were a shock to my system.

"You have my support, Simone." She laid her hand over my right hand, then reached across the table to take Brianne's, forming a circle. "I'm on your side."

"Good. Thank you. Thank you both." I blew out my breath and stood up. "We're clear."

Gumbo hopped on my chair, propping his front paws on the table. His claws matched his bow, a brilliant shade of blue reminiscent of the Blue Hoard. And the lightning that had flown from my hands.

He angled his wide-eyed gaze at Brianne. "I can haz?"

"No more, little one." She scratched him behind his ear while I scooped the fries off the table. Lauren followed me into the kitchenette, chewing on her lip like it was dessert.

"Um, I wanted you to know that Ray's weekly session is today. He'll be here soon." She checked her watch, even though I suspected she knew exactly how much time we had.

"I can handle it, Lauren." I paused to listen to my own voice. Sure enough, I could handle it.

"You know," I continued, turning to lean against the counter and face her, "it occurred to me the other day that you did me a favor."

"I did?" Lauren crinkled her eyebrows. "When?"

"Thirty years ago, when you told Ray that Ethan and I were sneaking around together and broke us up."

"Oh." She hung her head, yanking on her ponytail. "About that ..."

"No, I mean it." I waited until she'd looked up to continue. "Whatever your reasons were, because we both know you didn't believe Ethan and I had a thing, you did me a favor. I was going to choose him."

We walked into the lobby just as the front door opened. Ray strode in, halting when he saw the two of us talking. I hugged Lauren close, whispering in her ear in case Ray had super wolf hearing.

"The mistakes I made these past thirty years—and there have been plenty—they're mine. If we'd stayed together, I would have followed him. Chosen him. I got to choose me instead. Even if I didn't realize it at the time."

I pulled away, pausing at the door to my office.

"If I can screw up that powerfully without realizing it, imagine what I can do now that I'm paying attention."

CHAPTER THIRTY-TWO

"Oh my God, is this real?" I'd arrived at the boardroom thirty minutes early, and after a moment of deliberation, decided to keep my original seat. Ethan had followed me in, spoiling my plans to gather myself before everyone arrived. But since he'd given me the best news possible, I wasn't too upset with him.

"It's real." He pointed to one of the fifty arrow stickers on the stack of papers. "As soon as Brianne comes in, she can witness our signatures. He signed every single page. I made sure of it."

There was a gleeful menace to his voice that I had to admit I enjoyed, which made me feel incredibly guilty. My marriage of twenty years was about to end. I should have at least been sad about it.

But I wasn't. We hadn't spoken since the day he stumbled onto the Magnolia property and Ray chased him away. There was no indication he regretted his actions. He definitely hadn't tried to win me back.

"How did he look?" I *did* feel guilty about all the accidental hexes. Even if I'd cleared them.

"Completely normal, Simone." Ethan squeezed my hand in reassurance. "There was no trace or mention of cursing. He didn't dare say anything ill about you in my presence." He paused, his voice heavy. "He didn't even contest the divorce."

"Of course he didn't. I gave him everything in our house and the house itself." Maybe I was a touch bitter he'd let it go so easily. Even when you're meant to give up the past, it hurts to see it drift away like a passing storm.

I had to remind myself this was a good thing. He could have all the dated furniture and bad memories.

Everything I needed was here in the Magnolia.

Well. Almost everything.

My throat closed, but it wasn't a magical constriction. Whatever magic I had tried when I wrote Gabe a letter hadn't worked. Or worse, it had. Either he'd never read it and was still walking around thinking he didn't have a mother, or he'd read the letter, remembered me, and decided he wanted nothing to do with me.

Both options sucked. And both were out of my control.

I didn't realize I was crying until Ethan's fingertip grazed my cheek.

"Don't cry, Simone. It's going to work out."

Ethan didn't know about Gabe. If he did, he probably wouldn't be so gentle with me right now. He probably thought I was shedding tears over my marriage ending.

"Thanks, Ethan. You've been a really good friend through all of this." I leaned in to him, wrapping my arms tight around his neck.

He pulled back to meet my eyes, so close to me his breath was warm on my face. The tears still cascading landed on my lips, and I licked the salt off. Ethan's breath stopped. He inched forward, and in that inch, I forgot everything else existed.

He'd always been a good friend. Nothing more, right? Had I crushed on him in high school? I didn't think so. But now, whether I was ready for it or not, something new was developing.

He was so close. He smelled sweet, like a crisp soda on a hot day. His mouth was right there. To hell with it. I moved in.

Only the racket of approaching voices from the hallway stopped us. I yanked myself away before our lips could meet, all but vaulting myself to the drink cart for water. When Brianne and Gumbo entered, Ethan pretended to straighten the divorce papers.

"Brianne, good thing you're here." His voice had a tremor I'd never heard before. "We'll need you to be a witness."

Thirty minutes later, I was officially divorced and poised at the end of the table. When Lauren walked in, Ethan fled to her, and the two giggled at the opposite side of the room. Something flared inside me. Jealousy? I couldn't be sure, but it was a sensation I was not proud of.

Gumbo was asleep on my lap. I rubbed his chin, straightening his glossy black bow. He yawned and stretched, hopping onto the chair next to me when Brianne set a packet on the table.

"Ready for this?" She whispered as she placed the blank pages in front of me. I hadn't provided any information for the meeting, which made me curious where the information came from. It was yet another factor on my long list of things to figure out.

In the meantime, I trusted Brianne. She seemed to keep a tight ship, and since I didn't know what was broken, I wasn't about to go around fixing things.

"As I'll ever be," I answered.

The Twins arrived at the same time, their steps in sync, identical looks of insolence on their flawless faces. The air shifted. Something like a bubble of joy burst in my chest. This time, I recognized it as a spell. With a single glare at Lydia, it disappeared. She shrugged like an innocent child.

It was going to take a lot of work to get them on my side.

"Right. Everyone's ready." Brianne gestured at the Twins. "Shall we get started?"

Like our first meeting, the clock I'd never actually seen began to chime.

"Lydia Langley, Division Head for Magnolia Medspa." Lydia could not have looked or sounded more bored. She crossed her arms and placed both hands on the pages in front of her as if a water gun were pointed at her head.

The room lurched around me, the walls warping and extending in all four directions. Apparently their fae powers hadn't messed with the room. This was House's doing.

"Lyra Langley, Division Head for Magnolia Salon." Lyra had all but been a ghost since I arrived. I'd forgotten her voice was a melody. She blew me a kiss then repeated the cross-arm gesture.

The table and our chairs, with us in them, rose from the floor to float in the center of the room. The clock chimed again.

"You got this, Simone." Lauren whispered from her seat. Then, louder, she continued the ritual. "Lauren Whitaker, Division Head for Magnolia Physical Therapy."

Maybe roller coasters weren't that bad. The clock chimed. A strange, new sound followed. A kind of chirping, like a cricket hiding under a couch.

"Ethan Mosely, Lawyer pro tem for Magnolia Therapy and Wellness."

"Brianne Steele, Operations Manager for Magnolia Therapy and Wellness."

Gong. Chirp. Gong chirp.

"Gumbo. Ancient Archiver and Mystical Protector of Magnolia Therapy and Wellness." This time, Gumbo *did* sound ancient. Like a wise lion, I half expected him to hold his next-of-kin overhead and sing.

My pants vibrated. Why were my pants vibrating?

Around the table, a sea of faces I'd mostly gotten to know over the past thirty days stared at me with expectant expressions. I could see in them the beginnings of a new family. A family that wasn't without its struggles, but that would embrace me. A family that would celebrate my strengths and forgive my weaknesses.

If only my pants would stop vibrating.

"CC?" Ethan's wolfish grin filled my vision. "I believe your phone is ringing."

Oh. Duh. I fumbled my buzzing cell phone from my pocket. It wasn't ringing. Instead, there were a series of text messages.

From my son.

I only had to read the first one to know everything would be all right. But the second one soothed every piece of my soul.

Hey, mom, I got your letter. Let me know when you have a minute. I thought maybe I'd come visit this new house of yours before school starts again.

I love you.

I didn't bother to hold back the whoop of joy that erupted from my entire being. It wasn't everything. But damn it was a good start. I would fix things with Gabe. I'd continue to grow in my powers. I'd embrace all that it meant to be a word witch.

And I'd use everything I learned to help others feel as complete, empowered, and whole as I did in that moment.

For the first time, I noticed not all the chairs floated. A single chair remained on the floor, dozens of feet below us.

Agatha's chair.

Everyone at the table waited, their eyes on me.

I was ready.

"Simone Bardot, Division Head for Magnolia Mental Health and Supreme of Magnolia Therapy and Wellness."

Sure, my voice stalled a bit when I called myself Supreme, but I could handle that. After what I'd been through the past five weeks, I figured I could handle anything.

I crossed my arms and laid them on the paper. A title floated to the surface.

Magnolia Therapy and Wellness
Monthly Board Meeting

I turned to the first page. The words that appeared bolstered my confidence even further.

"Okay," I said to the room. "First order of business is the official transfer of power from Agatha Dupree, who has earned the right to rest in peace, to me."

The empty chair rose from the floor and rested on the center of the table. I could just make out her form. My heart swelled from her pride.

The air around me swirled like a hurricane, the noise a roar in my ears. A million tiny specks of light floated in the air, tossed like a buoy in the ocean, they danced around me. Bees swarmed in the light, which flashed green and blue.

Electricity lifted my hair to stand on end. I pulsed with it, like lightning incarnate. The sound of my own laughter echoed through space and time.

We landed on the floor with a thud. Agatha's chair trembled and jerked. Then it disappeared.

"Thank you, Agatha." I met each face at the table with a confident smile. I smile I felt from the inside out.

"Let's get started."

THANK you so much for reading *Witchful Shrinking*! If you loved the book and have a moment, a quick star-rating or review makes a huge difference in helping other readers decide if this is their new favorite series.

SIMONE'S new life has started out with a bang. Literally. A midnight explosion, threatening graffiti, and seemingly small disturbances warn Simone that she's can't get too comfy in the Magnolia just yet. Which would be manageable, if she weren't overwhelmed with every emotion on the earth. What's a middle-aged witch to do when she feels like a teenager?

^^^ Scan the code above or click here in your ebook to read book two, *Witchful Linking.*

WANT to sit in on Simone and Agatha's strange session, and the aftermath that ended Simone's marriage?

^^^ Scan the code above or click here to download your exclusive bonus scene, free when you join my newsletter.

ACKNOWLEDGMENTS

To my dearest Brianne, my real-life soul sister. I have always and will always admire your ability to use your voice, for yourself and others. I love you so much. There's magic in our friendship, and every day I thank the universe for helping us find one another.

And for my Sweet Teas. Thank you for your never-ending support. For lifting me up when I can't reach out. And for making sure I take steps toward my dreams. Even when I don't want to. I'm so grateful for both of you.

About Jen Lassalle

Jen Lassalle is a New Orleans writer of fantasy fiction featuring awkward and compassionate middle-aged females with light romance and found family friendships that empower heroines in inclusive worlds where magic exists and mystical creatures live among us.

When Jen isn't writing, she's hanging with her family and friends at a local park or coffee shop. She likes working out, which is kind of weird, loves yoga, and plays video games. Of course, she reads.

Jen and her husband have two kids. One is an avid competitive swimmer (which sucks up all their weekend time). The other is a daydreamer like Jen who plays Bowie on guitar and anime theme songs on his keyboard.

You can follow Jen's socials using the links below.

- facebook.com/jenlassallewrites
- instagram.com/jenlassalle
- amazon.com/JB-Lassalle/e/B0BFJXP4GC
- tiktok.com/@jen.lassalle

www.ingramcontent.com/pod-product-compliance
Lightning Source LLC
Chambersburg PA
CBHW060244030726
47493CB00025B/2214
9781961731141